se Geo   McSkimming was a boy he
found an old motion-picture projector and a tin
containing a dusty film in his grandmother's attic.
He screened the film and was transfixed by
the flickering image of a man in a jaunty pith helmet,
baggy Sahara shorts and special desert sun-spectacles.
The man had an imposing macaw and a clever looking
camel, and Geoffrey McSkimming was mesmerised
by their activities in black-and-white Egypt, Peru,
Greece, Mexico, S
other ex

Years later he discove
and has spent much of his time since then retracing
their footsteps, interviewing surviving members of the
Old Relics Society, and gradually reconstructing these
lost true tales which have become the enormously
successful Cairo Jim Chronicles.

To research *Cairo Jim and the Tyrannical Bauble
of Tiberius*, Geoffrey McSkimming followed in the
footsteps of Cairo Jim, Doris the macaw and Brenda
the Wonder Camel through ancient and modern-day
Rome, finding a story that was so unexpected, on
many occasions he had to have a good sit down and
a careful think about where to take the next step...

For Belinda

con tutto il mio amore

First published in Great Britain 2008 by Walker Books Ltd
87 Vauxhall Walk, London SE11 5HJ

2 4 6 8 10 9 7 5 3 1

Text © 2001 Geoffrey McSkimming
Cover illustration © 2008 Martin Chatterton

This book has been typeset in Plantin

Printed in Great Britain by
Cox & Wyman Ltd, Reading, Berkshire

British Library Cataloguing in Publication Data:
a catalogue record for this book is available from the British Library.

ISBN 978-1-4063-1047-4

www.walkerbooks.co.uk

CAIRO JIM

AND THE TYRANNICAL
BAUBLE OF TIBERIUS

A Tale of Ancient Atrocity

GEOFFREY McSKIMMING

WALKER
BOOKS

▲▲▲▲▲ CONTENTS ▲▲▲▲▲

A WORD TO MY READERS

Cairo Jim, that well-known archaeologist and little-known poet, used to say that History, like a fat man's overcoat, has many, many pockets – some of which are used frequently, others less so.

We know the whereabouts of a lot of things in the overcoat of History. We can still find the pockets where ancient things have been put and stored and remembered.

But there are other pockets in History's overcoat that we have forgotten about. In these pockets, over-looked by Time and regular use, are some awesome secrets from the past.

As I was told by Gerald Perry Esquire (Cairo Jim's patron and founding member of the Old Relics Society in Cairo), Jim, Doris the macaw and Brenda the Wonder Camel would probably have preferred that *some* of the neglected pockets of History's overcoat had remained zipped tightly shut...

If that had happened, however, then maybe the following story would not be here for me to tell...

G. McS.

Part One:

THE OLD
AND THE NEW

"Se non è vero, è molto ben trovato."
– Common Italian saying from the 16th century

("If it is not true, it is a happy invention.")

A MOONLIT NIGHT
AT THE FORUM ROMANA

IT ALL BEGAN, this strange succession of events, with a mighty shudder of the ground at the ancient ruins of the Forum Romana.

That was not all: there was also a noise – a huge din, a subterranean blast from something that sounded like an otherworldly, gravelly trumpet. It erupted from deep beneath the monuments and the broken columns and the white, headless statues in the Forum.

Up until this, the night had been still and calm. A weak moon had sailed forth across the skies over the city of Rome. The city had almost settled down for the night: there were not many cars or motor scooters on the streets, and no more than a handful of late-night restaurants and cafés were still open. Only a few people could be seen, wandering home after a big meal or a night out on the town.

But in the ruins of the Forum Romana there had been silence. A straggle of cats had sleeked haughtily around the place (as if they owned these ancient, crumbled buildings and overgrown gardens), but apart from them there had been no other signs of life.

The white statues that lined the derelict House of the Vestal Virgins stood on their pedestals, overlooking

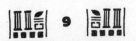

the narrow pond and garden, as they had done for over two thousand years. The after-midnight breeze rustled the ivy on the cracked walls and rippled the surface of the pond. Clouds travelled slowly across the sky, and moonshadows filtered across the Forum.

It had seemed as if it was going to be a night of deadly quiet.

Until...

GGGRRRRRAAAAAAAAAAAAHHHHHHHHHH HHHHNNNNNNNNKKKKKKKKKKKKKKKK!

The ground had moved, had buckled, as though it was trying to break itself apart, and the trumpeting had come – threatening but muffled, huge but somehow strained, as if it were being held back by something.

Some of the free-standing columns swayed infinitesimally. A few tiny cracks splintered the semi-circular facade of the Temple of Vesta. One of the statues at the House of the Vestal Virgins rocked forwards, and then back, on her pedestal.

It was a big enough tremor, and a loud enough trumpeting from somewhere far under the earth, far beneath the beautiful ruins, that it should have been noticed.

But no one had been there to observe or hear.

No one, that is, except for a single figure, half-shadowed in the gloom and moonshimmer. This figure had slipped into the Forum, swathed in the shadows that had travelled with the clouds far above.

In the tightly closed fist of this person was a small object from ancient antiquity, black as the darkest night and strangely shaped. Older than memory than most historians would allow.

It was being clenched so tightly, so forcefully, so *urgently* in this person's hand, that it could have been a minuscule star just fallen from the heavens...

If only that were all it *had* been...

HAT'S OFF

"RARK! MAYBE *THIS* WILL GET RID OF the stinkiness!"

Near the entrance to the Valley of the Kings in Upper Egypt, at the camp of that well-known archaeologist and little-known poet Cairo Jim, his devoted companion Doris the macaw was jerking up and down in a state of high flustration.

"Quaaaaoooo," snorted Brenda the Wonder Camel (Cairo Jim's other devoted companion) hopefully.

On a small portable table Doris waddled around the source of the stinkiness: Jim's brand-new pith helmet, which had only arrived the day before. Omar Dahling – the owner of the Omar Dahling Clementine Hat Shoppe in nearby Gurna Village – had imported the pith helmet all the way from India, from the world's best pith helmet maker.

It was a jaunty hat, with a broad brim and a crisp white cotton fabric covering the woven pith. The straps were made of the sturdiest leather and the underside of the crown had an attractive osnaburg lining with a bold design of miniature cumquats on it.

But it also stank.

Of kerosene.

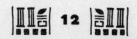

"Why d'you reckon they put *kerosene* all over it?" asked Doris, stretching her yellow and blue wings and jerking up and down some more.

Brenda swished her tail and had a think. "To keep out bugs and things while it was travelling all the way from India to here," she thought.

Being a Wonder Camel (the rarest and most intelligent breed of Bactrian camels in the known world), her thought travelled out of her head and into the mind of Doris.

"Rerk!" Doris screeched excitedly. "It's just dawned on me! They must've put the kerosene on it to keep out bugs and things while it was travelling all the way from India to here!"

Brenda fluttered her long eyelashes at her small friend.

"That *must* be the reason," Doris conjectured. "Why else would they do it? I mean to squawk, yesterday when Jim wore it, his eyes started running and he had a headache in no time at all."

"Let's see if your idea works," Brenda thought.

"Let's see if this will work," said Doris. She waddled around the pith helmet again – giving it a wide berth – to the other side of the table. There she had placed a bottle of Cleopatra's Whisper perfume which she and Brenda had just bought from the Scents and Sensibility Perfume Emporium in Gurna. "Let's do this before he comes out of his tent," she said in a quiet tone.

"Quaaaaoo," snorted Brenda, just as quietly.

 13

Doris used her beak and the tips of her wings to unscrew the bottle. She placed the lid on the table and put her beak over the open bottle. Immediately, she staggered back. "Reraaark!"

Brenda looked at Doris, who was blinking her eyes rapidly and shaking her head.

"'Soft, soft! It smells most sweetly'," she muttered, quoting from *Pericles* by William Shakespeare. "A little *too* sweetly, if you ask me. What do you think, Bren?"

Brenda took a step close to the table and, opening her nostrils wide, had a big sniff. Her nostrils and the hairs in her mane tingled as the strong odour of countless, oily roses swept over her.

"At least it's *strong*," said Doris. "If anything could smother the kerosene smell, this should do it."

Brenda snorted – now even her humps were tingling, and that was a sensation she never enjoyed!

"Quick, let's do it! I can hear Jim stirring in there!"

Brenda clamped her teeth gently onto the brim of the pith helmet and turned it so that it was upside-down. Doris picked up the bottle with one claw (trying to hold her breath at the same time), tilted it, and began sprinkling Cleopatra's Whisper around the inside of the hat.

"Ooh, what a stench! It's so sweet and ... rosy!"

"Quaaaaooo."

"Reminds me of Jocelyn Osgood,"* Doris said, the feathers around the edges of her beak crinkling.

"No," Brenda thought. "Her perfume is more like

a mixture of freesias and gardenias. And a bit of aviation fuel now and again."

"There we go," murmured Doris, still carefully sprinkling droplets of Cleopatra's Whisper all around the inside of the pith helmet. "This stuff should be strong enough to get rid of the pongiest of – RAAARK! WHOOPS!"

"Quaaaaoooooooo!" snorted Brenda in alarm.

For a second, Doris had relaxed her grip on the bottle and it had fallen into the pith helmet. Half of the oily perfume gushed and gurgled out of the bottle before Doris snatched the bottle out again and screwed the top back on.

"Quick," Brenda thought, her telepathic powers charging through her mind, "he's coming!"

"Erk! He's coming!" Doris's feathers started jiggling and she shoved the bottle to Brenda. "Here, Bren, go and bury this under some sand dune somewhere."

The Wonder Camel took it in her jaws – being careful not to inhale while doing so – and trotted off towards the nearby Valley of the Hairdressers.

Frantically, Doris fanned her wings over the pith

---

* The Valkyrian Airways Flight Attendant and Cairo Jim's "good friend" who sometimes accompanies Jim, Doris and Brenda on their archaeological assignments. (See *Cairo Jim and the Secret Sepulchre of the Sphinx* and *Cairo Jim and the Lagoon of Tidal Magnificence*.)

helmet, trying to waft the frightful odour of half a bottle of Cleopatra's Whisper away into the hot desert air.

Suddenly she heard footsteps behind her. In no more time than it takes to blink, she overturned the pith helmet so that it was once again sitting on its brim on the table. Then she turned to see Cairo Jim coming towards her, putting on his special desert sun-spectacles.

"Doris, my dear." He smiled – he always smiled that big, broad smile every day whenever he greeted both her and Brenda. (Even though the three of them had been together for a long time, he never failed to enjoy the first greeting of the day, as if it were the very first time they had met.)

"Salutations," she said, stiffening her spine and putting her wings behind her back.

"Where's Brenda?"

"Urm … she had to see a man about a cat."

Jim looked at her, puzzled.

"Only jesting. I think she took a wander."

"Ah." The archaeologist-poet reached out for his new pith helmet.

"RAAAAAAAAAAAAAAAARKKKKKKKKK!"

Jim pulled his hand back sharply. "What is it, Doris?"

"Don't put that on, Jim. Not yet, anyway."

"Why not?"

"Well…" She waddled to the edge of the table and then half hopped, half fluttered up onto his shoulder. "I was only thinking the other day how much nicer your hair would be if it were a shade or two lighter."

"Pardon?" Now he was really getting puzzled.

"Only a tad, mind you." She ran a wingtip over his freshly washed hair. "And the best way to do that is to get a bit of sun onto your hair."

"But, my dear, I'll get sunstroke if I don't wear my pith helmet. We don't want that happening again. Remember last time?"

"How could I forget? For three days you thought you were the King of Ethiopia."

"Haile Selassie," said Jim, frowning at the memory.

"Brenda and I bowed to you so much, our beak and snout were almost permanently acquainted with the sand."

"Yes, it wasn't a good time. Although I did write some different sorts of poetry while I had it."

Doris said nothing to that – there was nothing she would not do for Jim, except read his poetry.

"Now come on," he said, "let me put it on."

"No, no, no! What about the kerosene? You'll get another headache!"

Jim sniffed the air. "Can't smell any. But I *can* smell..." He crooked his arm and she hopped down onto it. "Doris, you're smelling especially fragrant today."

She blushed beneath her feathers. "Thank you," she prerked.

"*Very* fragrant."

"Jim, just wait a while before you put on your pith helmet. I'd like to see your face – all of it, your forehead

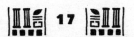

as well – just for this morning. Rerk. I mean, you cover your head so much, sometimes I can't remember what the top part of you looks like."

Jim was extremely puzzled but, because Doris was such a unique and quirky macaw, and because he respected her brilliance and her quaint ways, he agreed to her request.

"All right. I won't put it on until midday. Then—"

The insistent ringing of a bicycle bell interrupted him. He turned towards the roadway and he and Doris saw, coming from the direction of Gurna and pedalling earnestly, the Gurna Village Postal Representative.

"It's Quentin Turhan-Bey," squawked Doris.

"I wonder what he's got for us."

Brenda came lumbering back to camp.

"My lovely!" Jim gave her a huge smile. "Good morning."

"Quaaoo," she snorted, and snouted his arm – the arm that Doris wasn't perched on.

The bell on Quentin Turhan-Bey's bicycle was being rung so forcefully that it sounded as though it was about to fly off the handlebars. At last the bike skidded off the road and into the campsite.

Quentin Turhan-Bey – an agile man who was eighty-four years of age and a keen fitness fanatic – leapt off the bike, letting it clatter onto the sand. He sprinted across to Jim, Doris and Brenda and pulled a small yellow envelope from his wide leather satchel.

"Pyramids of good greetings to you," he puffed.

"I have an urgent telegram from the Old Relics Society in Cairo."

"Rerk, it'll be from Gerald Perry Esquire."

Quentin Turhan-Bey thrust the envelope at Jim, who took it and ripped off the end.

"Thank you, Mr T.," he said. He took out the telegram and quickly read the last line. "Yes, you're right, Doris. It's from our patron, Perry."

Quentin Turhan-Bey, not wishing to lose his pace but also wishing to know of the telegram's contents, started doing a series of energetic deep-knee squats in the sand with his hands on his hips. "Not bad news, I hope?" he huffed as he went up and down.

"As with most of Perry's communications," Jim said, "I really can't tell."

"*Talata, arba'a, khamsa,*" counted Quentin Turhan-Bey in Arabic, as he continued his squats.

"Quaaaooo," snorted Brenda, in a read-it-please-read-it sort of way.

Jim cleared his throat and read the telegram aloud:

PLEASE COME TO THE OLD RELICS SOCIETY AT ONCE STOP STRANGE HAPPENINGS IN ROME STOP I FEAR IT'S A MATTER OF ARCHAEOLOGICAL FELONY STOP AM SENDING A COPTER 11 AM ON THE SEVENTEENTH STOP MEET ME IN SOCIETY'S LIBRARY, BY SCULPTURE OF HEDY LAMARR STOP

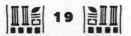

YOUR PATRON & FRIEND, GERALD PERRY ESQ STOP FINAL STOP WILL YOU PLEASE STOP IT NOW STOP NO I DON'T WANT TO SEND ANY MORE STOP THAT'S ALL I HAVE TO SAY TO THEM STOP WHEN I SAY STOP I MEAN STOP NOW LOOK I'M NOT PAYING FOR ALL THESE EXTRA WORDS STOP ENOUGH IS ENOUGH ALREADY STOP WHO'S IN CHARGE HERE STOP

"Some telegram operators," grunted Quentin Turhan-Bey, "are very persistent. *Tisa'tashar, 'ishrin, waHid wi 'ishrin*. Ooh, that's enough of *those*. Now for some push-ups."

"What's the date today?" Jim asked urgently.

"Seventeenth," thought Brenda.

"Seventeenth," announced Doris.

"And the time." Jim looked at his Cutterscrog Old Timers Archaeological Timepiece on his wrist. "Five to eleven. That doesn't give us much time, gang."

"*Itnein*," counted Quentin Turhan-Bey as his nose touched the sand.

"Rark, so he wants us to go to Rome?"

"Via the Society in Cairo. That's what it sounds like."

"*Arba'a*," grunted Quentin, lowering himself again.

Brenda raised her powerful ears, as a distant sound began to swell over the peaks of the dunes. "*That* sounds like a helicopter," she thought, as the noise of a huge propeller droned louder and closer across the sandhills.

And, sure enough, she was right.

ᖓᖓᖓᖓ 3 ᖓᖓᖓᖓ

AT THE OLD RELICS SOCIETY

"TO THINK," pondered Gerald Perry Esquire, "that a single bowling ball could lead to such distraction!"

The elderly, possum-faced gentleman was sitting in his favourite plump armchair in his favourite corner in the Old Relics Society's vast and cool Library. He was reading a small paperback novel entitled *Jives of a Bengal Dancer*. It was much thumbed, and the cover – which showed a young woman wearing an astonishing amount of feathers, doing the splits on a stage while blowing bubbles at the same time – was a little grimy, but Perry was enjoying it nevertheless.

Behind his armchair, high on a marble plinth, was a handsome head-and-shoulders statue of the actress Hedy Lamarr.

(She was not, of course, anything to do with the ancient world, but was greatly admired by many Members of the Society, who had held numerous pigeon raffles to raise the money to have the statue sculpted. Some of the Members were so taken with it when it arrived that they had spent days on end sitting in front of it, sighing loudly and falling asleep, and waking and sighing loudly, and falling asleep again and then waking and sighing, as they beheld

Hedy Lamarr's stony, severe yet eternally beautiful face and remembering the days when they had been younger men and she had not been set in stone.)

Gerald Perry turned the page, and his marsupial eyes grew wider. "Well, strike me down with a cantaloupe," he exclaimed, his moustache bristling at what he had just read. He looked around the Library and, when he was sure no one was nearby, he kept on reading.

Presently the echo of hoofbeats and footsteps filled the cavernous room, but Perry was so engrossed in *Jives of a Bengal Dancer* that he didn't hear anything.

The hoofsteps and footsteps came closer. Perry was just coming to a part in the book where Priscilla Zither, the heroine and Dancer of Exotic Jives and Jitterbugs, was having a nasty encounter with a man who stacked the tenpins at the Bogra Bowling Alley, when a softly spoken voice pulled him suddenly away from Bengal:

"Perry, it was a smooth ride in the 'copter, thank you very much."

Perry's head snapped back against the armchair. "Jim! Doris! Brenda! Welcome!"

"Quaaaaoo!"

"Rark." Doris, sitting on Jim's shoulder, blinked at Perry. "What's that you're reading?"

Perry quickly slapped the book shut and shoved it under the cushion of his seat. "Er, just a little … a small volume on … oh, never you mind, you inquisitive macaw."

Jim noticed how the colour had changed in Perry's cheeks, and he smiled.

"So nice to see you all again," the old man said. "Pull up a chair, Jim, and Brenda, you sit yourself on that bit of carpet there – I had Spong the receptionist buy it especially for you this morning at the Cairo bazaar – don't know why the wretched man went and got one with all those pink dolphins on it with those silly smiles, he's obviously got no taste at all – but still, it looks comfortable enough to me."

Brenda gave a snort of gratitude and lowered herself onto the gaudy square of carpet. When she was settled she gave Perry a big flutter of her eyelashes.

"So," said Jim, pushing a large armchair into place so that he could sit opposite his patron, "tell us what's wrong." He took off his pith helmet and laid it on the chair's wide arm.

Doris fluttered off his shoulder as he sat, and perched on the chair's other arm. "Yes," she prerked, "what're these strange goings-on in Rome you mentioned in your telegram?"

Perry took a big sniff of the air. "Goodness," he said, looking perplexed, "can you smell that? It's like a rose bush has suddenly marched in here."

Jim sniffed also. Doris looked at Brenda, and she at Doris.

"It does too," Jim agreed, screwing up his nose slightly. "Although it's more like a *hundred* rose bushes, if you ask me."

Perry winced. "It's enough to make m'moustache curl."

"The unexpected smell of mystery," mused Jim. "Maybe that's what it is. Here we all are, with something strange going on in Rome, a mystery most probably, and maybe this is what an unexplained mystery smells like. You know, like the saying 'the sweet smell of success'."

"Smells more like roses that've just been sick all over the place," Perry said, rubbing his moustache this way and that. "The sweet smell of *excess*."

Doris jerked up and down. "Forget about the smell! What's going on in Rome that you called us all the way up here for?"

"Eh? Oh, yes, let's get down to business." Perry reached over to a small side table and picked up a neatly folded newspaper. He opened it and turned to one of the inside pages. "Here," he said, handing the paper across to Cairo Jim. "Yesterday's edition. Wrap your peepers around that."

The archaeologist-poet took off his sun-spectacles and examined the page. "Well, swoggle me with a sundial," he said.

"Rark, read it out, Jim!"

"Quaaaaoo!" Brenda flicked her tail through the cool air.

Jim put on his reading-out-loud voice and did so:

"'TIME SKIPS A BEAT IN ROME'. That's the headline."

Doris blinked impatiently. "Read on, Jim!"

Perry crossed his legs and listened attentively.

"'In what appears to be a glitch in everyday happenings, the people of Rome are finding themselves utterly bamboozled by strange events.

'Last Thursday a man walking his dog along the Via Cavour suddenly found himself in the embarrassing situation of walking smack-bang into a brick wall. "I could have sworn I had just walked my terrier past the wall, because he stopped there for a moment to carry out some business," said a confused Stefano Reni, still sporting heavy bruises on his forehead. "But, no more than a few seconds later, I walked straight into the wall! Somehow I had turned around, without realising it, and BANG! And, at the very moment I crashed into the wall, my watch stopped. The watchmakers tell me they cannot get it going again."'"

Jim paused and frowned.

"So?" said Doris. "A man bangs into a wall and his watch stops. Maybe he was a bit squiffy or something. Just because of this we have to go to Rome?"

"Ah, but there's more," Perry said. "Read on, my friend."

Jim found his place and continued reading:

"'This is not the only instance of strange occurrences. The following afternoon, six newspaper vendors along the Via del Corso found, to their consternation, that they were all selling newspapers from the previous day. Yet that very morning, the newspapers they had been selling were current. All of the newspaper vendors were interviewed by police, and all of them claimed no knowledge of how the old newspapers came to be at their stalls.

All six of the newspaper vendors' watches have ceased to work and are unable to be repaired.'"

"Hmmm," hmmmed Doris.
Jim kept going:

"'In the outdoor coffee shops in the Piazza Navona, waiters have been sacked for serving customers empty cups – which many of them swear they had filled with hot coffee only seconds before. In other parts of the city, motor scooters are inexplicably stalling, their riders being catapulted over the handlebars onto the sidewalks. Cars, trucks and buses have been stalling for no obvious reason.

'These strange happenings are usually confined to several minutes in the early afternoons. The

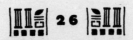

disruptions only last for moments, but are disconcerting enough to cause much trouble to those involved. In all reported cases, the people involved in such happenings have suffered breakages of their wristwatches.'"

Jim stopped. "That's the end," he said, shaking his head.

"Weird, wouldn't you say?" asked Perry.

"What on earth could be causing it?" squawked Doris.

Brenda rolled her head in a circle – she had no idea at all.

"You know what I think?" said Jim.

Perry squirmed, partly out of interest and partly because the spine of *Jives of a Bengal Dancer* was sticking up through the cushion into a place he would have preferred it wasn't sticking into. "Go on," he said.

"Well, said Jim, "I've a theory about cities. And it's this: when cities get too big and too old, they start to lose much of their reason."

Brenda swished her tail as she listened.

"Cities become chaotic in their old age and bustle. That's why," he said, "I prefer to live at our quiet campsite down near the Valleys of the Kings and Queens and Nobles and Hairdressers. When we're not travelling round the world for you, Perry, I mean. Down there, it's calm and easy and…" He trailed off, and a faraway look came across his face.

"Jim?" Perry leaned forward. "Are you all—?"

"I think he's got a poem coming on," Doris muttered, rolling her small eyes.

Jim's wistfulness had activated the poetry cells in his brain and, before anyone could stop him, he was reciting:

"Give me the sand hills near the Valley of the
       Kings,
where Time and all of History breathes and sighs
       and sings,
where mysteries lie buried so deep beneath the
       sand,
where Brenda snorts so calmly while Doris perches
       on her stand,
where a tent can be a castle and a plate can be a
       platter,
where I can wear odd socks and it never seems to
       matter,
where the sun will cast its shadows, a-glow and so
       pretty –
no, you won't get the same in any big city!"

In the ensuing silence, Doris rolled her eyes again, Brenda swished her tail and Perry made a strange sort of noise that sounded like he was clearing his throat of an unwelcome swallowing of sandpaper.

"Yes," said Jim, "cities are not my favourite places."

"You made that clear," Doris squawked, "from that little outburst!"

"Now look, Jim." Perry clasped his hands around his upper kneecap, and wriggled as *Jives of a Bengal Dancer* bent under his weight. "I do want you to go to Rome to investigate all of this. I'm sorry that big cities are not to your liking, but this is all far more serious than one's personal tastes."

"But what's it got to do with us?" Jim folded the newspaper and handed it back to Perry. "Doris and Brenda and I are an archaeological team. We're good at finding out about things to do with the ancient past, but all of this sounds a bit too ... *modern*."

Doris opened and closed her big wings. "Yes, Perry, Jim's right. It doesn't sound like the kind of job we're used to."

Perry's eyes twinkled. He picked up another newspaper from the side table and passed it across to Jim. "Read the headline," he instructed. "It's this morning's edition."

Jim did as he was asked. "'PLAGUE OF LOCUSTS INFESTS DOLLY PARTON'."

"No, not that one, the one near the bottom of the page."

Jim scanned down the page and, silently, he read the headline. In a second, the colour drained completely from his face.

FELONY!

"I HOPED THAT I WOULD NEVER LIVE to see this happen," Jim whispered gravely.

"As did I, Jim," agreed Gerald Perry Esquire. "As did I."

"Reeerark! See *what* happen?"

Brenda snorted urgently at Jim to read the headline aloud.

"'VALUABLE ANCIENT ARTEFACT MISSING – TIBERIUS' BAUBLE AT LARGE'."

"Tiberius' Bauble?" squawked Doris.

"The Imperishable Bauble of Tiberius," said Perry in a solemn tone.

Brenda the Wonder Camel shut her eyes and thought hard, scouring her brain for any reference she might have tucked away in there about this thing called the Imperishable Bauble of Tiberius. But nothing came to the front of her mind – no tidbits of information, no smidgens of facts, no images of the object itself.

"It's an ancient artefact that once belonged to the Roman emperor Tiberius," Jim explained.

"Old wartface," added Perry.

"It was housed for the last three hundred years or so

at a museum in Rome, and hardly ever put on display to the general public."

"Coo," Doris cooed. "Why not?"

"Because," answered Jim, "it was always reputed to possess an incredible power."

"Yes?" Doris said.

"Quaaaaaoo?" Brenda snorted.

"Tell 'em, Jim," said Perry.

"Well apparently, so the legend goes, the emperor Tiberius had this thing … this Bauble … made in about AD 36, and it was supposed to be able to give him more power over his enemies than any other emperor, pharaoh, king, queen, general or chief in the entire history of the world had ever been able to muster."

"Rark! What sort of power? Was he able to conjure up huge armies at the drop of a hat?"

"No, my dear, far greater than that. They reckon that with his Bauble, Tiberius had the power to control the *very seconds that make up time*."

"Quaaaooo!"

"Some people believe that he could manipulate time and make it his slave. He could stop it and start it again, whenever he wanted. This way he was able to dominate battles against his enemies, to win at whatever he set out to do, to conquer other nations and his foes with the minimum of effort and loss of life."

Doris blinked. "And these goings-on in modern-day Rome … oh, fluster my feathers!"

"Many people," Gerald Perry said, "have always felt

that the power associated with the Imperishable Bauble of Tiberius was nothing more than poppycock. They argued that it was impossible, that no tiny Bauble could have such astounding powers. But those of us who know the ancient world have always thought otherwise."

Cairo Jim nodded. "That's why the Imperishable Bauble of Tiberius has been kept away from the public for so long."

"Unfortunately," said Perry, "not for long enough. Now some underhanded thief has gone and grabbed it. According to that report in the paper, the Italian police have no idea who the thief is."

The minds of Jim, Doris and Brenda all had an instantaneous thought.

"Crark!" Doris flapped her wings. "Bone! Captain Neptune F. Bone! It's him, all right, you bet your life!"

"Quaaaoo," agreed Brenda, her nostrils flaring angrily.

Doris paced up and down the arm of the chair. "That corrupt, amoral, depraved, shady, profligate ratbag…"

"Who's tried to swindle us out of every discovery we've made," Brenda thought, her nostrils flaring wider.

"Who's tried to swindle us out of every discovery we've made," screeched Doris. "The miserable diddler! The lying hound! The huge great dollop of rottenness! The wannabe despot and deluded megalomaniac!"

"Not to mention the worst dressed man in the Society's annual fashion stakes," added Perry.

Jim shuddered.

"It's got to be him!" Doris jerked up and down so fast she was almost a yellow and blue blur on the arm of the chair.

"I would agree with you," Perry said, "if it weren't for one small detail: Neptune Bone is behind bars."

Jim's jaw dropped. "He's working *in hotels*?"

"No, no, no," said Perry. "He's in prison!"

"And about time!" exclaimed Doris.

"The Cairo Prison," Perry told them. "It seems he was turned over to the Antiquities Squad after a recent explosive incident in Sumatra."

"We remember what he did in Sumatra, don't we, gang?"*

"Too right." Doris scowled.

"Quaaoo quaaoo."

"Being who he was," continued Perry, "he was given a speedy trial, and convicted almost straight away. He's been there for the past month, all chained up in a solitary cell. So it can't have been Bone who stole the Bauble."

"Perry, I don't wish to be disrespectful, but I'll believe it when I see it. Bone's underhanded to the point of totality, but he's also brilliant. He's fooled us all in the past, as you know."

---

* See *Cairo Jim and the Lagoon of Tidal Magnificence – A Sumatran Tale of Splendour*

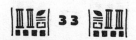

"Yes, yes, Jim." Perry had a bit of a squirm. "I remember the time he faked his own death and I believed it. I even announced his demise to a huge gathering here at the Society. The rotten rorter!"

"So this could just be another of his hoaxes. Another of his intricate schemes," said Jim. "What if he concocted the story that he's in prison, merely as a smokescreen so that he could go to Rome and steal the Bauble? No one would suspect a man in chains in the Cairo Prison, would they?"

"It'd be typical of Bone," thought Brenda.

"It'd be typical of Bone," said Doris.

"But he *is* there," Perry protested. "One of m'colleagues, an erudite chap by the name of Antonio Horgan, went and peeped through the hole in his cell door. He saw Bone, all chained up and looking very angry. Told me so himself."

"How long ago was this?"

"Couple of weeks. Shortly after Bone was thrown in there."

Jim thrummed his fingers on the top of his pith helmet, next to him on the armrest (an invisible burst of oily rosiness spread into the air as he did this). "Knowing Bone, anything might have happened since then. I wouldn't be at all amazed if he were free, and up to his repulsive habits again."

Gerald Perry Esquire sniffed and wiggled his moustache at the fresh onslaught of aroma. Then he gripped the arms of his chair and, in an agile movement, got quickly to his feet. "There's one way to put our minds at rest," he announced. "Come on, m'friends, we're off on a little excursion."

"Where to?" asked Doris.

"To the Cairo Prison. Let's see for ourselves if justice has finally caught up with that overblown brute!"

BONE ALONE

ON THE WAY TO CAIRO PRISON, in Perry's custom-made limousine (he had two others, but this one had been specially designed so that Brenda could fit in the back without her humps being squeezed as if she were an accordion), Perry let Jim, Doris and Brenda in on some of the recent gossip from the Old Relics Society and the world of archaeology.

"…and old Binkie Whiskin – you remember him, I'm sure, that man at the Society who has an unhealthy and all-consuming passion for finding and photographing snail shells—"

"Yes, we remember him," Jim said as the limousine moved jerkily through the crowded streets of Cairo.

"—well, he's gone off to Equatorial Guinea, where he's heard they've found a very old breed of snail with a turquoise-coloured shell that can whistle through its something-or-other… Whiskin did tell me about it, but I can't say I was all that interested."

"The only good snail is on a dish," squawked Doris, perched on Jim's knee. She had a well-known taste for Malawian snails, the juicier the better.

Brenda watched the bustle outside as Perry continued:

"And there's talk, Jim, that there may be some new excavations going on very soon up at Crete. Seems some of the Society's members think they may have uncovered something of interest at the Palace of Knossos."

"Now that'd be worth seeing," the archaeologist-poet commented.

"And there was something else I meant to tell you…" Perry took off his sun-spectacles and polished them with a natty osnaburg handkerchief while he thought. "Ah! I know! D'you recall that clever young woman you encountered when you went to Turkey? She worked for the Istanbul Branch of the Antiquities Squad."

Jim thought for a moment. "Yes, of course I do. She travelled with us when we were on the Artemis assignment."*

"Meltem," Doris said.

"Meltem Bottnoff." Perry nodded in an almost dreamy sort of way. "Well, I had word a little while back that she's left the Squad for good. Seems she'd had enough of trying to thwart felons and big corporations intent on plundering the ancient past. And she could never get her indoor plants to do well in that office she had."

"Goodness," said Jim. "How could anyone ever have enough of protecting antiquities?"

---

* See *Cairo Jim Amidst the Petticoats of Artemis – A Turkish Tale of Treachery*

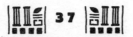

"Quaaaooo," came an agreeing snort.

"I s'pose," Perry said, "it's either in your blood or it isn't. Still, she was a smart and attractive person. I'm sure she'll get on in life. Oh! Did you hear about the special visitor we had a few weeks back?"

"No. Who was it?"

"The man who invented linoleum."

"Really?" Jim wound down the window a bit; the smell of oily roses was filling the limousine again.

"Oh, yes, and you'll never guess what he was wearing..."

And, as the limousine travelled to the Cairo Prison, Perry continued to regale his friends with a story the likes of which they had never heard before.

It was a small cell, and it reeked of some strange fishy odour: an odour that came from deep beneath the stone foundations of the prison, where the river Nile lapped its ancient water against the huge limestone pylons that supported the building, and at a place in the river where flotsam and jetsam and other things, things that had drowned or had fallen dead into the water, were regularly washed up.

In the corner of the cell furthest from the heavy steel door, Captain Neptune Flannelbottom Bone sat on his narrow, lumpy stretcher. He was decidedly unhappy.

The once-grandiose man had been stripped of all his bright and mismatched clothes when he had been admitted to this place. Now he wore only the prison standard-issue uniform of a coarse pair of trousers and a shirt that constantly made him itch. He cared not for the design of the garments, nor for the colours: a pattern of puce-coloured arrows on a faded grey fabric.

His immense stomach and fatty thighs bulged against the uniform as if they were trying desperately to escape the confines of the material.

Gone were his fez, his emerald-green waistcoat, his plus-fours trousers and his bold stockings. Gone were his grimy spats, which had always covered his feet. Now his feet were bare – bare and itchy – and around his ankles were two heavy chains which attached him permanently to the back wall of the cell.

Gone, also, was his cigar case, which had been chock-full of his favourite Belch of Brouhaha cigars. His craving for those was almost agonising.

The only thing he had persuaded the prison guards to allow him to keep had been his gold fob-watch. He had claimed – very shrilly – that it had been a present from his beloved mother, and that he would surely die in this place if they did not allow him to keep it with him.

A weak, pale light came through the tiny window, high up in the wall. This window was barred, heavily and formidably.

The large, fleshy man had found, the week before, a flat piece of stick. He had rubbed it back and forth against the stone wall until it had become smoother. This smooth piece of stick he was now using to buff his

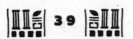

finger nails, as he thought about freedom, wealth and professional manicure services.

"Arrrrrr," he muttered deeply. "To think that I, the boldest and most ambitious of archaeologists ever, should end up in a dump like this."

(He had found that muttering aloud to himself helped him to feel less forlorn, and besides, he had always enjoyed the sound of his own voice.)

Carefully he buffed the underside edge of his index fingernail. "Here, where humanity has ceased to exist. Here, where the stench is like being in the belly of a whale who has not cleaned his teeth for a decade. Here, where I have only my grandeur for comfort."

He lifted his chubby left ankle as far as the heavy chain would let him. "I'd have to be Herakles or Charles Atlas to be able to break these confounded things. Arrrr."

He lowered his leg and continued to buff and stroke his nails. Back and forth, back and forth, up and around and back and forth. As he did so, his resolve to escape grew stronger.

He began thinking about what great things he had (almost) achieved in the outside world. He thought about all the places he had been, all the wondrous ancient treasures that he had (nearly) discovered and stolen for his own personal profit.

He pondered all the wondrous ancient treasures that still lay on the outside, waiting for someone like him, someone with a great and far-reaching vision, someone who would never be curbed or hindered by the law or by good manners or decency. Those silly little distractions that would always be there to try and stop a Genius such as what he was.

As he contemplated all these things, a song began to form in his head. Without realising that he was singing, the words began to tumble out of his flabby lips, in time to his manicuring:

"I'm the last of the brilliant bad men,
my Genius knows no bounds!
They might've shoved me in this prison
– my ambitious desires have merely risen!
I'm a big achiever, a breathtaking deceiver,
If I could reach it, I'd steal the moon.
This prison cell, with its fishy smell
I'll be saying bye-byes to soon.
You can keep your bland politicians,
their villainy's not worth a dime;
they try to swindle – oh, come right off it!
They've no *idea* how to turn a profit!
But I'm the last of the brilliant bad men,
I'm growing badder all the time!

"Yes, I'm the last of the brilliant bad men,
there's none can hold a match to me!
My current unfortunate incarceration
is but a *temporary* situation!
I still have all my glory. My wonderful life story
shall continue when I've left this dump.

And when I'm free, just wait and see,
I'll make the whole world jump!
You can take your boring bankers,
what do they know about greed?
They try their rip-offs – their customers rave and
    shout –
when *I* swindle men, they feel they've had their
    gizzards taken out!
Arrrr, I'm the last of the brilliant bad men,
MY BRILLIANCE THE WORLD SHALL HEED!"

He would have continued, but at that moment the fingernails-down-the-blackboard sound of a key turning in the lock of his door made him throw down his manicure stick and clamp his hands over his ears. "Heavens to the Goddess Betsy," he cringed. "Is it cocktail time already?"

The door juddered open and Bone's guard – a wide-shouldered man named Qara, with three teeth, and about the same number of hairs on his head – stepped into the dinginess.

"Good afternoon," said Bone, scowling. "Come to take me to the hairdressers? Or is it Tuesday? Oh, yes, of course, you're going to give me that foot massage you've been so looking forward to."

Qara smiled, displaying two-thirds of his teeth. "Mr Fatmouth," he said in a deep, gravelly voice, "you have visitors." He jiggled the wide ring of keys that hung from his belt.

Bone stood and smoothed down his grotty uniform (he quickly scratched himself in a place not worth mentioning). "Well, don't just stand there like some hideous life-infested statue, show them in, show them in!"

Qara stared at him for a few seconds, then said, "If all those words tumbling out of your fat mouth were gold, I would be very rich man. Wait one moment!"

He exited, and Bone's head filled with the thought that he was about to be pardoned, and that the visitors waiting in the corridor outside were the Prison Governor and his Head Warden, come to apologise and to grovel and to promise him compensation – about a million Egyptian pounds – for locking him away when all he had tried to do was to alert the world to his own magnificence.

He was as wrong as he had ever been.

With a springy step, Gerald Perry Esquire came in, followed closely by Jim of Cairo with Doris on his shoulder and Brenda the Wonder Camel behind them (she could only manage to poke her head and part of her neck around the door of the tiny cell). They were accompanied by the unmistakable smell of wild roses and kerosene.

"And here is where your doings have led you," said Perry, eyeing the high, dank walls and the overblown man in his shabby uniform.

"Arrrr," sneered Bone. He screwed up his bulbous nose at the odour that had invaded his cell. "I thought

I detected the reek of unmitigated goodness and cheerfulness."

"Bone," said Jim. "Justice finally got you."

"About time," squawked Doris, blinking at the dishevelment before her.

The large, fleshy man plonked himself down on his stretcher. His ankle chains clanked heavily as he shifted his feet. "What, come to gloat, have you? Come to take a few piccies for the Society's pathetic little newsletter?"

Brenda clamped her nostrils shut – the mixture of roses, kerosene and fish was making her humps feel very strange.

"I know I'm seeing this through my own sun-spectacles," Jim said, "but I can still hardly believe it. Neptune Bone in jail."

Bone stared up at them through his hairy eyebrows (which resembled twin, overfed caterpillars who were too lazy to crawl off his forehead). "All because of those dreadful women from the Turkish Women's Olympic Championship Tent Erection Team."

"*They* put you in here?" asked Perry. "But I thought the Antiquities Squad got you."

"Four of those uneducated brutesses from the Turkish Women's Olympic Championship Tent Erection Team sat on me all the way back to Cairo. Then they handed me over to the Antiquities Squad. The rest, as they say, is what we all strive to uncover."

"It was quite a court case," Perry said to Jim, Doris and Brenda. "Swift and blazing. There was so much evidence against Bone, the judge threw the book at him."

"Not just the book," Bone growled, "she threw the whole wretched *library*. Arrrrrr."

"No more 'undivulged crimes, unwhipped of justice'," Doris quoted.

Jim looked at her.

"Rark. From *King Lear* by Mr Shakespeare. Act Three, Scene Two."

"Very good, my dear."

Bone rolled his eyes. "Oh, please, spare me the literature. And spare me your hideous glows of goodness." He pressed his back against the damp wall behind him. "You've come and got your jollities, now why don't you all skip away and help some little old lady across some street? And while you're at it, you could all fall under the wheels of a steamroller or some other unforgiving vehicle."

"We didn't come to gloat," Perry told him.

"No," said Jim. "We came because we thought you might've been involved in this." He took the folded newspaper from the pocket of his extra-wide Sahara shorts and handed it to Bone.

"What?" He snatched it from Jim's hand, and his eyes quickly sleered across the page. "Well, poor old Dolly Parton. She probably had it coming, though."

"No, not that bit," said Jim. "The headline below it."

Bone's eyes widened, slowly and curiously, as he read the headline: "'VALUABLE ANCIENT ARTEFACT MISSING – TIBERIUS' BAUBLE AT LARGE'."

He looked up suspiciously. "Is this true? This isn't one of those stupid joke newspapers which people get printed for ridiculous occasions or to fool their friends, is it?"

"It's absolutely true," spluttered Perry. "I certainly wouldn't waste m'hard-earned money on such silliness!"

Bone sneered at him. "So saith the man who has invested his hard-earned money in the establishment of a chain of forty-seven take-away pigeon restaurants across northern Africa."

"Forty-six," Perry muttered. "There was that spot of bother with the one in Heliopolis."

"Don't ever mention *salmonella* to him," Jim whispered to Doris. "Or Flambé Pigeon Combo."

"Rark."

"Tiberius' legendary Bauble," Bone murmured, remembering the few things he had studied about it when he had been a student at Archaeology School, many years ago.

"No, Bone," Jim said, "it's not a fake newspaper."

"It's the real macaw," Doris added.

"And," said Perry, "we only came here to ascertain that you haven't had anything to do with it."

"As if I could," Bone glowered. "If only I weren't here in this forsaken place..." For a second, his eyes flickered, as though two fiery snakes had slithered behind his eyeballs. "The Imperishable Bauble of Tiberius. What a theft! Arrrrr!"

"And now that we're sure you aren't the culprit,

we'll leave you." Perry began to shepherd his friends out the door.

"With pleasure," added Doris.

Jim paused, taking a long, last look at his most determined enemy and erstwhile thwarter. "Goodbye, Bone," he said finally. Then he put on his pith helmet and left also.

"Good riddance," hissed Bone when they had gone.

Before he locked the huge door, Qara peered in. "So, Mr Fatmouth, your visitors not stay for very long, huh?"

"Get out, you toothless, hairless, charmless thing, you! Go and listen to your Shirley Bassey tapes and leave me in peace!"

"Gladly, Mr Fatmouth. That for me will be *great* pleasure."

"The Imperishable Bauble of Tiberius," repeated Neptune Bone in a tone of extreme envy. "To think that someone purloined *that*."

TO ROME

"BLOW IT!" EXCLAIMED JIM, as Perry's custom-made limo sped towards Cairo Aerodrome.

"Quaaooo?" snorted Brenda.

"Rark, what's up?"

Jim patted the pockets in his shirt and shorts, and then picked up his knapsack from the floor and started rummaging around inside it. "I must've left that newspaper in Bone's cell."

"Never mind, m'boy," said Perry, tapping him on his sturdy kneecap. "Y'can buy another when you land in Rome."

"Yes," said Jim, putting the knapsack down again. "Didn't Bone's cell stink? Fish and dampness and rotting roses or something."

Doris and Brenda looked at each other, but squawked and snorted nothing.

Perry asked, "Now that we know Bone's not involved, where do you think you'll start looking when you get there?"

Cairo Jim wound down the window and stared out. "I've been thinking about that. We don't have much information to go on with this one—"

"You can squawk that again!" Doris said.

48

"But I think I know the best place to start. Perry, did you ever meet my old Professor of Italian Antiquities from Archaeology School?"

Perry rubbed his moustache back and forth. "Er … was he the man who could change a light bulb with his nostril?"

"No," said Jim. "Not that I'm aware of."

"Oh, you'd be aware of this, for sure. I went to a party once, and this man was there and somebody said: 'Did you know that whatsisname can change a light bulb with only his nostril?', and everybody said: 'No, now that's a thing you don't see every day', which was not really right because this party was being held at night, y'see, but anyway, we all agreed that we should like to see this man perform his speciality and so we took out the light bulb – I remember, young Norma Scott burnt her fingers very badly, had t'put 'em in a pat of butter for the rest of the night which made her very popular with the cat, I can tell you, but she kept dropping things thereafter – where was I? Oh, yes, we took out the light bulb and gave it to this man, and d'you know what he did? I've seen things in m'travels, but I'd never seen *this* – he took this new light bulb and he pushed it right up his—"

"No, Perry, I think you're recalling someone else. No, my Professor of Italian Antiquities was a very neat and fussy man. He would never have done such things with his nostrils."

"Ah." The possum-faced gentleman sat back in the

leather seat and clasped his kneecap. "Go on, then, Jim, tell me about him."

"His name is Pasqual deLirio," Jim said. "He had – still has, I suspect – an encyclopaedic knowledge of ancient Roman history, and the legends associated with it. He was very enthusiastic. A little *too* enthusiastic, some of my fellow students thought."

"Nothing wrong with a bit of enthusiasm," Perry said. "If there was more of that in the world, I dare say we wouldn't have hindrances like bank queues and paper cuts. Not to mention polka music."

Brenda and Doris gave each other puzzled looks (sometimes they couldn't follow Gerald Perry's ways of thinking at all).

Doris blinked at Jim. "So where is Pasqual deLirio these days?"

"He retired early, and went to Rome to live. It was a natural choice, what with his absolute passion. He's now a sort of honorary curator at a museum there. The Palazzo Altemps it's called."

"The Palazzo Altemps," repeated Perry. "Now where've I heard of that place? Hmmm. Can't quite recall. Never mind." He leant forward and tapped loudly on the glass partition that separated them from the chauffeur. "Garth! Garth! Would you mind turning on the radio? I think we could do with some music back here."

"Very good, sir." Garth, the always-smiling and ever-hearty chauffeur, obligingly turned on the radio.

The sound of a newsreader's voice burst into the limousine.

"…in Rome, where further pandemonium took place yesterday afternoon. Traffic along the Via del Tritone came to a standstill when a large bus full of German tourists became stuck after all eight of its tyres deflated simultaneously. People walking in the street reported other incidents or unusual events, including one man whose belt suddenly became so horrendously tight around his waist that he gained an extra four centimetres in height, and a woman who found that somehow she was wearing a pair of men's shoes which she had never before seen in her life…"

"The Imperishable Bauble of Tiberius," thought Brenda. "What on earth is this thief up to?"

Cairo Jim started to perspire. "The Imperishable Bauble of Tiberius," he said to his friends. "What on earth is this thief up to?"

"Crark! I'm back!"

Neptune Bone looked up to the barred window. There, perched on the ledge like some tatty, feathered gargoyle, was a gloating raven. Its eyes throbbed the colour of blood.

Bone stared at the bird impatiently. "You certainly took your time, you tardy, tattered twerp."

"Gratitude, gratitude, gratitude," croaked the raven, who went by the name of Desdemona. "In all the years

I've been hangin' about with you, it's a wonder I haven't been overwhelmed by your thanks and appreciation."

"Spare me the drivel. Did you get what I told you to get?"

"Yep." She stepped aside, to reveal a small mobile phone on the ledge behind her. "I nicked it from a Coptic priest when he put it down for a second to twiddle his beads." She pecked quickly at a chomping flea that was dining under her wing.

"Well don't just sit there like some deformed miniature newsreader, give it to me!"

"For you, oh Thief of Ragbag, anything." She kicked it off the ledge and into his pudgy hand. Then she soared off the windowsill and came to sit on the far end of his stretcher.

"I have absolutely no time to waste, now that certain new information has come to my attention."

"Eh? What sort of information? Has Qara been tormenting you with his Shirley Bassey tapes again?"

"No, you foolish flying fermentation of futility. No, while you were away, I was unfortunate enough to have a visit from Gerald Perry Esquire with Cairo Jim and his pathetic, wholesome duo."

"Was that *macaw* here?"

"Arrr," arred Bone, trying to work out the buttons on the mobile phone. "And the humped monstrosity."

Desdemona's black-as-pitch feathers hackled, and the countless fleas concealed within bit her more ferociously. "That gaudy, smartyfeathers macaw! Ooooh, one o'these days I'm gonna get my talons on her, and then it'll be goodbye, Miss Gold-and-Blue and hello, Miss Plucky-plucky-baldy!"

"These wretched modern things … what's this button for?"

"Her and her bright plumage … I'll change all that, you wait and see. Nevermore, nevermore, nevermore!"

"It was my visitors who gave me this new information." He thrust the newspaper at her while he continued trying to work out how to turn on the phone. "There, get a beakful of that!"

She scanned the front page with her throbbing eyes. "Ha-crak-har! Hope they mess up her hair for ever!"

"Not the Dolly Parton bit, the other bit!"

Desdemona read the article, slowly and stumblingly, to herself. When she had finished, she belched loudly.

"You mannerless mess of muck."

"Thank you."

"Did you understand what you just read? Did you comprehend the hugeness of the event? Did you get how absolutely important this theft is, and why I am now positively itching – much more urgently, and not just because of this uniform – to get out of this stinking prison?"

"I always thought a bauble was something you make in the bath after you've eaten too many baked beans."

Bone looked at her as though she were the dimmest thing this side of midnight. "You disgusting, deadbeat of a d—"

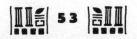

He was interrupted by a series of digital notes that burst from the mobile phone. "Arrr, look, Desdemona, the lights are on!"

"Crark." She hopped closer to him and stared curiously at the phone.

Bone punched in some numbers, and held the phone to his hairy ear. As he listened to the ringing, he stroked his beard and his scheme swelled ever wider in his mind.

"Who're ya ringing?" asked Desdemona.

"An associate who owes me a rather large favour. His name is Leslie Swaddling. He owns the Pneumatics Inflatable Apparatus Company here in Cairo, and he – hello, is that Leslie Swaddling?"

Desdemona heard a noise through the phone that sounded like someone was massaging themselves with a pot scourer.

"Bone here. Neptune Bone."

The pot-scourer noise became louder and much more scratchy.

"I do not think it would be in your interests to hang up on me, Lessie. After all, you owe me a big favour."

The pot-scourer noise was so loud it sounded like it was rubbing away an entire skyscraper.

"Settle down, settle down. You *do* owe me, Lessie old boy. Remember the time I gave you that tip about the Malayan Futures Market? You made a positive stash on all that rubber, yes?"

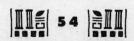

The noise on the other end went a bit quieter for a moment, but then returned, louder and scratchier than ever.

"Arrr, that's not my fault, Lessie. I didn't twist your arm to manufacture four million latex ice-cube containers. I can't be held responsible if people don't like the taste of rubber in their cocktails, can I? Or if you almost went broke?"

"Losers," muttered Desdemona.

"So," said Bone, keeping an eye on the door in case Qara began opening it, "are you going to do me this small favour I am about to ask? Before you answer, let me advise you that I happen to have, in a locked location somewhere of my own knowing, evidence that links you with the bankruptcy of a Southern Patagonian nudist colony. And it wasn't just a case of *frozen assets*."

The pot-scourer noise screamed down the line.

Bone continued, "Now I know for a fact that you are soon seeking election to the position of President of WORMIE."

"Wormie?" croaked Desdemona.

"The Worldwide Organisation of Rubber Makers Incorporated Everywhere," Bone hissed out of the side of his mouth. "Isn't that so, Lessie?"

Desdemona heard only silence on the other end.

"And if I were to let this information about the nudist colony fall into the hands of the other members of WORMIE, then I think your chances of becoming

President would be about the same as Mary Queen of Scots rising from the grave to do a spot of stenography. Do you get my meaning?"

The pot-scourer noise came back, but to Desdemona it sounded almost tired.

"Arrrr," gloated Bone. "I knew you'd see things my way. Now listen carefully: here is what I would like you to make for me, and deliver it here before ten o'clock tonight. A large, life-sized, perfectly realistic..."

As the raven listened to her companion's bossy tones, she rolled her throbbing eyes and wondered what sort of outrage he was about to perpetrate *this* time.

"And don't skimp on the latex eyelashes, Lessie, or I'll be coming after you. Arrrrrrr!"

ᕼᕼᕼᕼᕼ 7 ᕼᕼᕼᕼᕼ

BLOWING UP THE DIVA

AT CAIRO AERODROME, Gerald Perry was shaking Cairo Jim's hand with earnest precision.

"Now be careful, Jim. I know I must've said this a hundred times, but the Society's only got the one of each of you, and our Members all feel that you three are irreplaceable."

"Thank you," said Jim. "We'll go with caution."

"And with ever-open eyes," squawked Doris on his shoulder.

"And," thought Brenda, "with our minds clear and ready."

Her thought pervaded Jim's head. "And," he said to Perry, "with our minds clear and ready."

Before them on the tarmac, Perry's silver Ford Tri-Motor plane was waiting.

"The pilot is aboard, so you'd better go, before he turns on the propellers." Perry began walking with them across the tarmac. "Now I've arranged everything in the plane. There's a nice comfy place for Brenda to sit, with some more dolphin-patterned carpet, I'm afraid."

"Quaaaaoo," she snorted thankfully.

"And some special Malawian snails in a bowl for you, Doris."

 57

"My thanks be with you always, Gerald Perry," cooed the macaw.

"And this is for you, Jim." He handed Jim a large envelope. "Some Italian lire and a map of greater Rome and some other bits and pieces to get you going when you're over there. And there's something else."

He reached into the pocket of his white linen blazer and pulled out a long piece of string. He handed this solemnly to Jim. "Remember the first motto of the Society: 'You never know when you'll need a good bit of string.'"

"As usual, Perry, you're a champion."

"Yes," said Perry, who knew it as well as anyone.

At the foot of the stairs leading up to the plane, Perry turned to Jim, Doris and Brenda. "I hope you find this thief, swiftly and without any trouble. It's wrong, Jim, terribly wrong to use a thing from the ancient past to steal the very seconds of time away. It's against nature, that's what it is."

Jim nodded, Doris blinked and Brenda flicked her ears in agreement.

"Time," said Perry, "is always precious, especially when you get to be my vintage." His possum-like eyes clouded and the wrinkles around them deepened. For the tiniest of moments he looked every bit his age.

"Don't worry," Jim advised. "We'll do as well as we can."

Perry looked at him carefully, and the old sparkle instantly returned to his eyes. "Of that, like poppies in springtime, we're always assured."

With no more fuss they said their goodbyes, and Gerald Perry Esquire watched as his friends climbed aboard.

"Fight the fight," he said quietly to no one in particular as the plane started to trundle down the runway. "And stop this gross obstruction of what is meant to be, before the whole world gets tilted off its axis."

Bone was sprawling on his stretcher, like a great exhausted slug after a night of slime-making and too much eating, when a small object fell onto his head with a CLUNNNNK!

"What in the name of Icarus?" he growled, sitting upright and rubbing his greasy locks.

"It's that book you told me to steal," came Desdemona's hoarse voice from the window. *"Ventriloquism for Fun and Profit in Confined Spaces."* She swooped down and perched at the foot of the stretcher.

Bone picked up the book and scratched his belly. "The sooner we're out of here, the better. This uniform is making me so itchy I'm almost wearing my fingerpads away."

"I'm not surprised," said Desdemona. "There's such a lot of you to scratch, you could employ a team of four men full-time just for that very job."

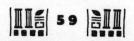

"Enshut your beak, you fetid foul flutterer." He flipped open *Ventriloquism for Fun and Profit in Confined Spaces* and read through the index. "Arrrr, this will do very nicely for the task at hand."

"What? What task at hand? When does the package from that Leslie Swaddling arrive?"

Bone pulled out his gold fob-watch and peered at the dial. "That slow little man. It's nine-thirty now. I told him to have it here before ten. Qara goes off duty at ten-thirty." A bead of sweat popped out on Bone's brow. "That Swaddling had better not stuff this up, or he'll be very *very* sorry."

Desdemona pecked a flea off her wing and spat it onto the cold, tiled floor.

"Oh, Desdemona, how I abhor being cooped up like this! What a humiliation for one with such natural born grandeur and brilliant foresight such as myself! How degrading for a Genius of such unrivalled and breathtaking vision such as what I am! What a complete and utter—"

There was a louder CLUNNNNK! and another object landed on his head: a wide, flat box bearing the colourful label of the Pneumatics Inflatable Apparatus Company of Cairo.

"Ha-crark-ha!" sniggered Desdemona, pecking at a circle of fleas on the back of her leg.

Bone rubbed his head again. "At least he packed it in a box that would fit through those bars," he grumbled.

"Let's get her out, then," Desdemona urged. "I can't *wait* to see *this*!"

On and on, as the plane speared through the cobwebby clouds in the dark, dark sky, the propellers blasted their constant drone.

On and on, as the inside of the plane's cabin dipped and straightened again, Doris tried to suck up her special Malawian snails without spilling any.

On and on, as the wings cut through the wisps of night so high above the ground, Brenda concentrated hard, trying to remember anything she had read in her calfhood about the Imperishable Bauble of Tiberius.

On and on, as the rhythm of the propellers and the engines and the bumping of the turbulence buffeted him in his seat, and as the mysterious smell of oily roses and kerosene wafted all around him, even here, Cairo Jim thought and pondered and looked forward to making contact with Pasqual deLirio as soon as they had landed in Rome. And, while all these things were filling his head, the poetry cells in his brain began to be activated.

Before he realised it, a poem had formed. With a thoughtful tone (slightly bewildered too, for he never knew how these verses came to him), he recited it aloud:

> "Tiberius, how serious
> your Bauble has become!
> Did you know, so long ago,

just what you had done?
Tiberius, oh hear me thus,
you've left a legacy
that might unravel all of us
and might lead to the fall of us
and may result in stalling us
and all our History…"

Doris shuddered, but said nothing – partly not to hurt his feelings, but mostly because her mouth was stuffed with snails and, as any sociable macaw knows, it is very bad manners to squawk with one's beak full.

"Atta boy, blow, blow, blow!"

Desdemona was enjoying the sight of Neptune Bone gasping for breath as he was trying to inflate the specially made item he had ordered from the Pneumatics Inflatable Apparatus Company: a life-sized, fully realistic rubber ventriloquist's model of the famous singer Shirley Bassey.

Next to him, on the stretcher, Desdemona was holding *Ventriloquism for Fun and Profit in ConfinedSpaces* open on page six. She cackled cruelly at Bone's efforts.

He took his lips from the model and his eyes from the book, and glared hatefully at the raven. "Stop gloating, you loathsome lump of laughter."

"Why? I haven't enjoyed m'self so much since you got your beard caught in the escalators when you were bending over doing up your—"

"Enshut it!" He wiped the perspiration from his brow and out of his moustache. "Consider yourself fortunate that you are unable to perform this task!"

Her rough, yellow tongue whipped out and she ran it delicately around the outside of her beak. "Not with these razor-sharp choppers. I'd have that thing ripped to tatters in seconds."

"Arrrr."

Desdemona's eyes throbbed thoughtfully, and her intense hatred for all women human beings rose up inside her. "Actually, that's not a bad idea. When you've finished with her, give her to me for two minutes, will you?"

"There shall be no time to spare once I have utilised the services of Leslie Swaddling's creation," Bone puffed. "That stupid man! Fancy forgetting to include a small pump!"

"Maybe he did it on purpose. Maybe he thought you could get rid of a bit of all that hot air inside you."

Bone took a deep breath. "If time were not conspiring against me, I would make you a sore and eternally sorry raven, you worthless wimp of woe."

"Promises, promises!"

Quickly he pulled out his fob-watch and checked the time. "Only seven minutes before Qara finishes for the night." He looked at the pile of rubber at his feet, and frowned.

The top half of Shirley Bassey stared up at him, half blown-up and lolling on her side. The lower half was still a flattish rubber mass.

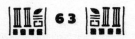

"Better get a move on, then," croaked the bird.

Bone put the fob-watch on the stretcher, next to Desdemona, and pressed his lips back to the model. With huge huffs and then huger puffs, he continued inflating.

Shirley Bassey's left arm slowly filled with air. One by one, each of her fingers plopped out from the round rubber palm.

Then her right arm started to fill.

The sweat was pouring off Bone's forehead and running down his back, soaking into his uniform and turning it a darker shade of grey.

He kept blowing, with one eye on Shirley Bassey and one eye studying the special alphabet in *Ventriloquism for Fun and Profit in Confined Spaces*.

Gradually the air moved downwards and Shirley Bassey started looking much more lifelike.

His cheeks were red with the strain as Shirley Bassey's left ankle swelled delicately. Then her foot took shape and her toes emerged, like tiny, beautiful creations, from her little toe all the way to her hallux.

"Crark! Three more minutes! Move it, Balloon Boy!"

"Confound that Swaddling man," gasped Bone. "Of all the places under the sun, why did he have to put the nozzle *here*?"

ONE MAN'S PASSION

THE KEYS SCREECHED in the lock. There was a loud CLICK, and Qara heaved open the door.

"So, Mr Fatmouth, my shift is up." He poked his head into the candle-lit cell. "I leave you once again to the watchful eyes of Mr Pretty, who will be here shortly."

(Mr Pretty was the night guard – it was his real name, and one he was forever trying to live down on account of the trouble it caused him so often in the prison.)

Qara waited for the usual smart-chappie sort of reply he always got from Bone whenever he bade him goodnight, but tonight there was none. The guard took a step into the cell. "Mr Fatmouth?"

Qara raised his small lantern. There, laid out on the stretcher like some scruffily clad beached whale, was Neptune Bone. His eyes were shut and a noise which sounded like a cross between a cannon blast and a sock full of custard being slapped against a tree was blurting loudly from his lips.

"SSSSQQQQQQQUUUUUAAARRRRRLLLLLLLLLLCCHHHHCCHHHH!"

Qara lifted his lantern higher, and ran its light across the prone man. "Some snorer," he said quietly to himself.

"He would wake the dead, if the dead were not so particular."

"SSSSQQQQQQUUUUUAAARRRRRLLLLLLL LLCCHHHHCCHHHH!"

At the second snore, Qara shuddered and turned to go. But he was stopped in his tracks by a voice purring from the darkness at the other end of the cell.

"Where do you think you're going, gorgeous?"

Qara shone his lantern into the darkened corner. His eyes widened, and widened some more, and would have kept on widening had not his eyebrows come to the spot on his forehead where any more widening of his eyes would result in injury to his neck.

"M ... M ... Miss ... B ... Bassey?" he stammered.

"The one and only," came the silken purr.

Qara stared, amazed and awe-struck at the sight of his idol, who was leaning casually against the wall. Leslie Swaddling had dressed her in a very tasteful black sequined cocktail frock, and it sparkled out at Qara and his lantern like a million stars that had unexpectedly swept into the dark, dank confines of the Cairo Prison.

"SSSSQQQQQQUUUUUAAARRRRRLLLLLLL LLCCHHHHCCHHHH!" snored Bone.

"This is not real," Qara muttered. A heavy frown spread over his lips, and his heart started beating uncertainly.

Here, in front of him, in the dingiest and most lonely cell in the whole prison, stood the greatest singer he had ever heard. But how? How could it possibly be?

"You must be a mirage," Qara said. "Like out in the deserts."

"I'n no nirage. I'n real, all right. You det your life."

"SSSSQQQQQQQUUUUUAAARRRRRLLLLLLLL LLCCHHHHCCHHHH!"

Qara turned and shone the light at Bone, who still lay fast asleep, with his flabby lips parted only slightly. Then he shone it back at Shirley Bassey (the beam was wobbling by now).

Then, slowly, he shone it again at Bone. "You cannot trick me, Mr Fat—"

"What's he got that *I* hathn't?" asked Shirley Bassey.

"Oh!" gasped Qara, who had not seen Bone's lips move at all. He swung the beam back at Shirley Bassey. "N .. n .. nothing, Miss Bassey. But … may I ask … I *have* to ask: how did you get in here?"

"I an Thirley Dathey. I can do anything, can't I?"

A bead of sweat popped out on Qara's forehead, and his heart started beating the rhythm of "Too Close for Comfort", which was his favourite Shirley Bassey song of all time.

And, because the life of a prison guard at the Cairo Prison is what it is, and because miracles seldom occur in such confinement, and because Qara was a hopeless romantic who did indeed believe that Shirley Bassey could do anything, he let himself be swayed completely.

"SSSSQQQQQQQUUUUUAAARRRRRLLLLLLLL LLCCHHHHCCHHHH!"

Qara ignored the disgusting noise from the stretcher.

His lantern beam bathed Miss Bassey in its trembling light, and he knelt before her.

"Oh! Oh! Oh!" His voice, instead of being low, was high and excited. "It *is* you! What an honour to at last meet you! I am your biggest fan in Egypt, Miss Bassey! I have every one of your records, and I am President of the Lower Egypt Shirley Bassey Fan Club and Singalong Society. I cannot believe you are here! Oh!"

"It's ne all right. In the thlesh."

Qara beamed, brighter than the light from his lantern. "I can see, now. Oh, Miss Bassey, for the first time in more years than I can remember, my heart is singing with joy!"

"I'n glad thor you. Yeth, Kara, I know oth your tassion thor ne. I hath heard oth this thron nany teotle."

Qara sighed.

"That is why I hath cun here tonight. To see ny nunder one than."

"Yes, Miss Bassey, I *am* your number one fan!"

"Dut thirst, tlease take oth your delt."

"M ... my *belt*?" said Qara. "You want me to ... take it off?"

A small breeze wafted through the opened door, and Shirley Bassey nodded. "Yeth. Tleathe. Thor ne. You thee, I hate theeing nen wearing delts. I think they are tho ugly. Tho unnethecary."

Qara looked down at his belt.

Shirley Bassey purred quietly: "I always theel it ith too *thornal* when a nan wearth a delt."

Quickly, Qara put down the lantern and undid his belt with all his prison keys attached to it. He dropped it on the floor behind him.

"SSSSQQQQQQUUUUUAAARRRRRLLLLLLL LLCCHHHHCCHHHH!"

"Thank you, Kara," said Miss Shirley Bassey. "Now, it theens I an at a dithadthantage."

"Why, Miss Bassey?"

"Well, you know thuch a lot adout *ne*, dut I know nothing adout *you*."

Qara blushed. "But I am simple man, Miss Bassey—"

"Call ne Thirley, tleathe."

Qara caught his breath (now his heart was beating "Too Close for Comfort" more forcefully than ever). "You would not be interested in the story of my humble life, surely, Shirley?"

"Go ahead," said Shirley Bassey, her head rocking back and forth in the breeze. "I'n all ears."

"Well, Shirley, I was born near the village of Deir el-Medina, about 65 kilometres west as the ibis flies…"

As Qara began to tell his idol all about himself, he was so transfixed by the sight of her, and he was concentrating so hard on making his life seem not too dull and unexciting, that he was totally unaware of what was taking place in the cell around him.

He did not hear the rustle of feathers as several keys were unhooked from the ring on his discarded belt.

He was not conscious of the occasional

SSSSQQQQQQUUUUUAAARRRRRLLLLLLLLL CHHHHCCHHHHs that blurted from the stretcher.

He was oblivious to the CLICK of the locks on Neptune Bone's ankle chains, and to the creaking of the stretcher as Bone swung his feet to the floor and sat up.

But there was one sound he *did* hear: a faint *hiiiiiissssssssssss* that seemed to be coming from the wall next to Shirley Bassey.

"Miss Bassey?" he asked, worriedly.

"Yeth? I'n listening. Tleathe go on, Kara."

The *hiiiiiiiiiissssssssssss*ing grew louder, and Shirley Bassey's head started lolling down onto her right shoulder, which was lowering itself slowly towards the floor.

"But you are... " Qara stared, his mouth dropping open. "You are ... *shrinking*!"

"Quick!" snarled Neptune Bone from behind Qara. He slapped the ankle chains around the guard's ankles and slammed the locks shut.

"What in the name of—?" Qara spun round, as Shirley Bassey *hiiiiiiiiiissssssssssssss*ed her last, and sank squashily to the floor.

Bone stood above the almost hairless, almost toothless man. "Arrr. Now the roles have been reversed, you wretch!"

"Ha-crark-HA!" gloated the raven.

"You won't be getting far, Fatmouth! I call help!" Qara opened his mouth to yell for Mr Pretty, but Bone was too quick: with a flash of his wrist, he pulled off one of his socks, threw it to Desdemona and, as had been previously arranged, she shoved it fiercely into Qara's opened mouth.

The stinking, sweaty sock filled his mouth completely, and his jaw was frozen wide open. His eyes darted back and forth, terrified at what might happen to him and nauseated by the taste and smell of what was crammed into his mouth.

"Now," Bone hissed at Qara, "lie still and don't even *think* of trying to escape. And, if you get in my way in the next minute, well … let's just say that your moronic, Bassey-loving face will be *much* more comfortable for me to stand on than this stone floor."

"You tell him, my Captain," Desdemona gurgled.

Bone grabbed her by her throatfeathers.

"SCCCCCRAAAAAAAEEEEEERKKKKKK!" she sccccccraaaaaaeeeeeerkkkkkked.

"Listen to me, Desdemona: I'm going to grant you your little wish. As swiftly and as savagely as you can, go and rip the semblance of Shirley Bassey asunder. But be careful – make sure that you slit the rubberware precisely, straight up and down each side."

He let go of the bird, and her eyes throbbed at him, blood-red in the gloom. "Like openin' a can of sardines, ya mean?"

"Arrrr. Don't damage the front or back. I need to slip the rubber on to disguise myself so that I may walk boldly out of this hell-hole."

"There's so much of you, you'd need a hot-air balloon

to cover all that flesh," she thought. But she said nothing, and hopped across the floor to the deflated singer.

"And," warned Bone, "don't touch those eyelashes, whatever you do!"

Desdemona clacked her beak open and shut. Then, in a blur of greasy feathers and bright yellow saliva, she serrated the rubber and started hopping all around it, her razor-sharp mandibles slicing through it as if it were warm butter.

"That's the way," whispered Bone. "Now, puncture the rubber where the eyes are. I need to be able to see."

With two savage stabs, Desdemona did as she was commanded. When she was done, Bone picked up the limp, airless rubberware. He quickly draped it over his head and shoulders. "Not a bad fit, what do you think? I must be very, *very* quiet when, as Shirley Bassey, I glide out of here."

"It'll be the silence of the hams," muttered Desdemona, staring at his overblown stomach making the cocktail dress stick out at a bizarre angle.

"Now, Desdemona, fly out the window and meet me in thirty minutes at the Big and Snide Men's Shop on the corner of Tahrir Square. We'll break in and get me my usual refined clothing and a tasteful fez or two, and then we'll make a raid on the Exotic Cigar Emporium. I can't wait for a Belch of Brouhaha!"

"Aye, aye, my Captain." She fluttered up to the window ledge, squeezed through the bars and, with a beat of her wings, melted into the gloom of the night.

Neptune Shirley Bassey Bone reached down and snatched up all the rest of Qara's keys on the wide ring. "I'll just lock the door on my way out, so you won't get too warm. And also so that Mr Pretty, when he finally arrives, won't be able to unlock the cell, because you won't have been able to hand him the keys."

Qara squirmed, but there was no way he could speak or disengage his jaw or get the heavy locks undone on his ankles.

Bone's crazed eyes peered out from under Shirley Bassey's rubber eyelashes. "Just you be a goody-goody little guardy-guardy and stay down there, all meek and mild. That way you might just inherit the earth. *I*, on the other hand, will inherit what shall be rightly mine: unimaginable domination of the world and all the wealth and glory that goes with it, thanks to a certain missing Bauble and a great abundance of my Genius! So long, Mr *Loser*!"

AT THE PALAZZO ALTEMPS MUSEUM

IT WAS EARLY IN THE MORNING in Rome, and still very dark, when Brenda the Wonder Camel cantered along the northern end of the Piazza Navona and up to the courtyard wall of the Palazzo Altemps Museum.

"Whoa there, my lovely," said Cairo Jim, bringing her to a stop by the enormous front doors.

"Quaaaooo," she snorted, her nostrils opening to breathe in the cool night air.

"Brrrrrr," Doris shivered, perched on the pommel of Brenda's saddle. Her crestfeathers stood on end, and her wings were jerking in and out against her back.

"Are you cold, my dear?" asked Jim.

"No, no. Just a little … *creeped*, I suppose."

"Creeped?"

"Rark. When we were coming along that Appian Way, the moon was shining down through all those old, old, trees, making all those shadows everywhere in the gloom. It was spooky, and I can't get it out of my mind."

Jim reached forward and patted her wing. "Don't you worry about it," he soothed. "It's no wonder you found it a bit like that. The Appian Way used to be the ancient Roman cemetery, you know."

"It felt as if the night were calling: 'Graves, yawn, and

yield your dead!'" Doris quoted from *Much Ado About Nothing*.

Jim shuddered at the poetic but gruesome image.

"Quaaaooooo," Brenda snorted quietly. Then she had a thought. "Isn't it a bit early to be calling on Professor deLirio? Won't he be asleep?"

Doris picked it up. "Isn't it a bit early to be calling on Professor deLirio, Jim? Won't he be asleep?"

Jim smiled. "Ah, I don't think so. Professor deLirio always suffered from insomnia when I knew him at Archaeology School. He told me he would sometimes go for five or six days without sleeping."

"Cooo."

"Quaaaoo."

"I bet he's still up and wandering about this museum right now. Even if he's not – even if he's tucked up safe and snug in bed with his eyes shut – we still have to knock on the door. This Bauble business is urgent, and the sooner we start to unravel it, the better for all the world."

"Knock on the door then," Doris urged him. "Go on, grab that big brass knocker and bang it!"

"Before I do," Jim said quietly, "there's something I should warn you about Professor deLirio. As I said before, he's always been an enthusiastic man, an *incredibly* enthusiastic man, especially when it comes to Roman antiquities. But there's something you should know about him before you meet him, so that the both of you don't get a shock."

"Spill the beans, then," Doris squawked.

"Quaaaaooo quaaaaaoooo," Brenda urged.

"Well, you see, it's like this: Pasqual deLirio has a type of … a kind of … well, he's got a very unusual *voice*."

Doris turned around on the pommel, to face Jim. "What sort of voice?"

Brenda curved her long neck and looked at Jim, her eyes full of curiosity.

"It's an *excited* voice," Jim answered, after thinking about it for a moment. "A *very* excited voice. It doesn't matter what he's saying – whether he's ordering a coffee in a café, or hailing a taxi, or whispering something into a telephone – his voice is always high-pitched, and he places a sudden emphasis on certain words. Almost as if he has a charge of electricity running through his voice.

"And," Jim added, "it's loud. Some people don't know if he's about to cry at you, or laugh at you, or just collapse from his enthusiastic energy. You know Jocelyn Osgood?"

"How could I forget?" squawked Doris, rolling her eyes.

"Well," said Jim, "she met Professor deLirio once, and d'you know what she said to me afterwards? She said that when he talks, he sounds like he's always got some part of his body on fire, and he can't put the fire out."

Brenda's mane quivered.

"Another person I knew, way back at Archaeology School, used to say that whenever she shut her eyes and listened to Professor deLirio in a lecture, it was like listening to someone who was forever stuck in one of those huge revolving doors in a city skyscraper."

"Some voice," Doris said.

"I just thought I'd let you both know," said Jim, reaching for the brass knocker. "Just so you don't get too startled."

He pulled the knocker towards him – it was cold and heavy and stiff on its hinge—then, with a big effort, he pushed it firmly back onto the door.

A loud *knockkkkk* echoed around them.

Half a minute passed…

Jim repeated the motion another three times. Another three echoes sounded, lingering into the still night.

In silence, Jim, Doris and Brenda waited. It was chilly out here on the doorstep, and Doris wrapped her wings around herself and lowered her beak towards her chestfeathers.

Then, after the last echo had disappeared into the void of the past, there came another series of sounds: a clanking and scraping and a high-pitched exclamation that was muffled on the other side of the door.

Presently these sounds came to a stop as well.

Doris looked up at Jim.

Jim looked at Doris.

Brenda looked at Doris.

Doris looked at Brenda.

Jim looked at Brenda.

Brenda looked at Jim.

Jim raised his eyebrows.

Doris opened her beak, then closed it again.

Brenda clacked a hoof on the marble step.

There was silence on the other side of the door.

Doris looked at Jim once more.

Jim gave a nod.

He reached forward and was just about to grab the knocker again when the door was wrenched wide open and, from the candle-lit gloom on the other side, a loud, piercing, wavering voice shot out at them:

"JIIIIM! JIIIIM OF CAIIIIRO! I AM SOOOO GLAAAD YOU HAVE COME!"

The owner of the voice was a tall, slender and still-youthful-looking man with dark, lustrous hair and a neatly trimmed, pencil-thin moustache. He wore a beautifully pressed cream silk shirt, a floppy silk bow tie patterned with small mauve cats, a red vest and a pair of sharply creased charcoal-grey trousers with the tiniest pin-stripe. His shoes were black as the night and as reflective as mirrors.

"I had a HUNCH you would be showing up to me," he said. "Come inside, per favore." His voice was a little more subdued now, but still sounded like a quiet fire alarm nevertheless.

"It's good to see you again, Professor," Jim said, jumping from Brenda's saddle. He led her by her halter into the Palazzo Altemps courtyard.

"You MUST call me PASQUAL, per favore. We are no LONGER Professor and STUDENT, si?"

Jim nodded. "Let me introduce my friends and

colleagues, Pasqual. This is—"

"Ah, JIIIIM, there is no NEEEED for these introductions. I have been READING about all of you in all the ARCHAEOLOGICAL journals for at least the last DECAAAAAAADE. There have been MANY photos of the THRRRREE of you in *Thoth's Blurter* and SIMILARRRRR publications."

Pasqual gave Doris (who was now sitting on Jim's shoulder) a wide, warm smile that made his pencil-thin moustache splay upwards. "Doris, the intelligent EXPERT on many ancient forms of writing and communiCATION. I welcome you to the Palazzo Altemps."

"Rark." Doris held out her wing, which Pasqual shook gently and courteously. "It's a pleasure to meet you, sir."

"And," Pasqual said, his smile growing wider and his moustache splaying further out towards his high-boned cheeks, "Brenda the WONDER Camel. Beast of wisdom and ancient secrets. I welcome you also."

Brenda's eyelashes fluttered of their own accord, and she swished her tail in a flattered manner.

Professor deLirio led the trio across the huge, cobbled courtyard and then through a tall doorway into a winding corridor.

"I am taking you to my QUAAAARTERS," he told them. "We will be more comfortable there, away from all these marble statues and REMNANTS of what I often call a somewhat WONKY past."

As they went along the corridor they passed many rooms which led off it. All of the rooms were lined with ancient marble statues, of men, women and children, and sometimes even animals such as dogs or turtles.

Doris and Brenda looked into as many of these rooms as they could, and noticed that in each of the rooms a single candle was burning in a small, wide bowl that had been set on the floor in the centre of the room. The candles did not provide much light, but from what Doris and Brenda could see in each of the rooms, the statues there looked unusual.

Doris fluttered from Jim's shoulder onto the top of Brenda's head, in between her ears. She lowered her beak and whispered to Brenda. "Do these statues look weird to you?" she asked.

Brenda moved her head in a small circle – she had been thinking the same thing.

"There's something about them, even in this light," Doris whispered. "Something not quite right. Too dark to see why, though."

"We may find out more when daylight comes," Brenda thought.

"Let's not worry about it tonight," Doris said. "We may find out more when daylight comes." She hop-fluttered back onto Jim's shoulder.

Brenda gave a snort and kept walking.

They came to a wide, marble staircase that led down into the cooler depths of the building. Pasqual stopped and sniffed the air. "STRRRANGE," he said, so suddenly and loudly that Doris (despite Jim's warning earlier) dug her claws into Jim's shirt, and Brenda let out a snort.

"What's strange, Professor?" asked Jim.

"Have a smell," said Pasqual.

Jim, who had grown used to the odour of the kerosene and oily roses, looked bewildered. "I don't smell anything unusual," he said.

"There is SOMEthing … something that doesn't beLONG here," said the Professor. "Something too SWEEET! Ah! I hope to Romulus that some of the statues aren't going the way of so MUCH ancient marble!" He frowned at Jim. "You know, the deterioration. This smell is the same sort of smell I have encountered at MANY ancient places where the marble IS AGEING very BADLY!"

He took another sniff, shook his head, and led them down the stairs. Brenda and Doris exchanged glances.

"I think you have an idea why we've come," Jim said as they reached the bottom.

"Of COURSE I have an idea," blurted Pasqual. "The Imperishable BAUBLE of Tiberius!"

Cairo Jim nodded gravely.

Pasqual took a small set of keys from his vest pocket and inserted one into the lock of a big oak door. "COME, come! Into my RRROOOOMS! There we shall disCUSSS this terrible situation at length, and attempt to work out what we can DO to try to avoid the CATASTROPHES to COME!"

SURFACE OF A LEGEND

"THERE IS NOT MUCH of ANYthing we can do at this hour," Pasqual deLirio informed them. "All of the reported BOUTS of this CHAOS in all the public places have happened in the afterNOONS, for a few minutes somewhere between the hours of one and three o'clock."

"As we've read in the papers," Jim said.

"Since the first outBREAK of this strangeness, I have been REGULARLY patrolling the streets between these hours. I suggest that the four of US do the SAME this afternoon."

Jim nodded, and Doris flexed up and down on his shoulder.

"In the meantime," said Pasqual, gesturing to a long, faded chaise longue, "per favore. Make yourselves like you are in your OWN HOME."

Cairo Jim thanked him, and sat on the chaise longue. Brenda lowered herself onto the floor at one end of the chaise, and Jim unbuckled her saddle.

"Rark," rarked Doris. "You have a pleasant apartment here, Professor."

"GRRRRAZIE!"

Doris jerked at his sudden response and watched

as he sat in a well-padded armchair and crossed his long legs.

Because the apartment was partly under the stairs, one end of the living room was much taller than the other end, which dwindled away to the height of a small chest of drawers.

"This is my READING room," Pasqual told them. "I also have a BEDroom and small BATHroom and KITchenETTE. It is very COMfortable, and enables me to CARRY on with my work, right here in the CENtre of ROMA."

One wall of the reading room was lined with bookshelves, which were filled with volumes and volumes of old books and journals. Some of them were stacked neatly in piles or standing spine-out, but most of them were sprawling on the shelves, as though Pasqual had picked up one book, had started reading it, then had shoved it back wherever he was standing and had then picked up another book or a magazine or journal, and had started reading that. This in turn had been replaced on the shelf in the same haphazard way.

As well as the chaise longue and the armchair, there was a small table (with a teetering pile of books on it), a footstool with a brocade covering, a tiny electric heater, several photo albums on the floor in the corner, a pile of recent newspapers, a painting of the Forum Romana as it would have looked 2000 years ago, and an ancient marble bust of a Roman man, which sat in a small recess in the wall behind Pasqual's chair.

Jim lifted Doris from his arm and placed her next to him on the chaise longue. "So," he asked the Professor, "have you witnessed any of these happenings out there for yourself?"

"No, no, NO!" Pasqual threw up his hands. "I have not been in the right place at the right TIME. ROMA is a big CITY, you know."

"Quaooo," snorted Brenda, swishing her tail.

"But," continued Pasqual, "I have been PINpointing the activity. It seems that the area where all of these inTRUsive actions are happening is bordered by THREE main thoroughfares, all of WHICH are in the centre of ROMA."

Brenda twisted her neck back and, with her dexterous Wonder Camel teeth, she undid one of the buckles on the left saddlebag attached to her saddle. She snouted around within and pulled out the map of Rome that Gerald Perry Esquire had given Jim before they had left Cairo.

"Good thinking, my lovely," said Jim, taking the map from her teeth. He spread it out on the floor in front of him.

"What are the streets that form the border?" Doris squawked, as Pasqual leaned forward in his chair and studied the map.

Jim took out his Pinpoint the Past, the Present and Your Freezer Bags Indelible Archaeological Felt-Tipped Pen and got it ready.

"The goings on," Pasqual told them, "have been

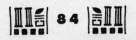

HAPPENing in an area south of the Corso d'Italia…"

Jim drew a line along the Corso d'Italia.

"And NORTH of the Via del Circo Massimo…"

"Rark, down there, Jim!"

The archaeologist-poet drew a line along that avenue as well.

"And bordered to the EAST," continued Pasqual, "by the Via CAVOUR…"

Jim traced the felt-tip along that street.

"And to the west by the River Tiber," Pasqual concluded.

Jim drew a long, serpentine line along the streets that lined the river.

Doris blinked at the map. "All roads lead to Rome, as they say."

"As you can SEE," said Pasqual, "it is a big area, but not TOO big to walk around in several HOURS."

"And how much of the area have you covered?" asked Jim.

"Oh, I would say ALL of it, at least TWICE over. But, as I said, I have not been FORTunate enough to be in the RIGHT place at the right TIME. So far the spectacles have ELUDED me."

"Strength in numbers," Doris said, opening and closing her wings and flexing the muscles under her feathers. "You know what I think?"

"What, my dear?" asked Jim.

"This afternoon," the macaw said, "when we all go out to see what's going on, I think the four of us should split up. We could each take a part of the area separately and try to cover that part fully. That way we've got four times the chance of seeing what might happen, haven't we?"

"Good thinking!" Pasqual deLirio slapped his knee.

"Four sets of eyes are better than one," cooed the macaw.

"Yes, Doris, only there's one thing."

"What, Jim?"

"Well, Brenda *could* go out by herself, but what if she's the one who finds what we're looking for? She can't speak with us, remember? How would she tell us what she's seen?"

(If only you knew, thought Brenda the Wonder Camel.)

"Rark. Hadn't thought of that. OK, I tell you what: Bren and I'll stick together. What say you, Bren?"

"Quaaaooo," snorted Brenda, who knew that sometimes the deepest truths should never be revealed.

"And," said Cairo Jim, "maybe the Professor and I should stay together. Until I get my bearings."

Pasqual sat back, his eyes bright. "That still gives us TWO times as much CHANCE of FINDing this unusualness," he said.

Jim looked pensive. "Professor—"

"PASQUAL!"

Jim, Doris and Brenda jumped.

"Pasqual," began Jim again, "do you know for a fact that these strange and potentially dangerous goings-on have anything to do with the theft of the Imperishable Bauble?"

"I would bet ALL of my ACADEMIC career on it," answered Pasqual deLirio emphatically. "There can be NO OTHER possible explanATION!"

"There's a lot I don't know," Doris prerked. "All this stuff about the Bauble. What's going on, exactly?"

Jim leaned forward and addressed his former Professor. "Please, Pasqual, there are many things we don't understand. I know that you, with your voluminous knowledge of all things to do with the ancient Romans, would have some extra information about the Bauble. Things that we're not aware of. Can you tell us more?"

Brenda shifted her legs beneath her, and gave Pasqual a look of keen interest.

"I most CERTainly will try to enLIGHTEN you," said Pasqual, settling himself back in his armchair. "There is a legend – and you and I KNOW, Cairo Jim, that LEGENDS are inextrICABLY entWINED with ARCHaeology – but let me START at the BEGinning…"

ROCK OF EGERIA

CAIRO JIM scratched his left kneecap and readied himself to hear the legend of the Bauble, while Doris blinked and got her wings into a comfortable position for listening.

Pasqual crossed his pin-striped legs the other way, and commenced: "In order to beGIN to get an UNDERstanding of the IMPERISHable Bauble of TibERIus, we must go back to the time of Numa Pompilius, the second king of Rome. He ruled over Rome from 715 BC to 672 BC, and it is he who first set aBOUT the sequence of EVENTS that formed the BAUBLE.

"There is a LEGend that Numa Pompilius introDUCED religious worship into Roma during his reign. It is SAID that he was TUTored in this AREA by a nymph that he had disCOVERED in the WOODlands. This NYMPH was named Egeria."

"Egeria," repeated Doris, quietly.

"Being a nymph," Pasqual continued, "EGERIA lived for a VERY long time. She OUTlived Numa Pompilius, and many other RULERS of the ancient empIRE. By the TIME the Emperor Tiberius took the THRONE, in AD 14, Egeria was renowned as the

EXPERT on all things RELIGIOUS and MYSTIcal."

"Ah," said Jim. "I remember now: Tiberius was heavily into astrology, yes?"

"Si," said Pasqual. He stood and went around behind his chair to the bust in the recess of the wall. "Here is Tiberius, HIMSELF," he said, running his elegant hand around the base of the bust's pedestal.

Jim, Doris and Brenda leaned forward and scrutinised the lemon-coloured marble sculpture of Tiberius. He had a neatly carved haircut, with a line of short curls peeping over the top of his marble forehead. His blank eyes were of a pleasing almond shape; his mouth, slightly pursed as though he were just about to tell someone to go away and leave him alone. His chin was weak, but his jawline was strong, and his hooked nose was a darker coloured marble to the rest of the sculpture. His ears were yet another colour of marble.

"Si," said Pasqual, "the ancient Emperor TibERius. You will notice that SOME parts of the bust are made from different marbles from the rest. This is beCAUSE this BUST has been reCONstructed. There are many such reconstrUCTED SCULPTURES and STATues here in the PalaZZO ALTEMps Museum. But I shall tell you about the MUSEUM later.

"Si, Jim, you are corRECT that Tiberius dePENDED heavily on astrology. He especially USED the foreCASTS of the STARS and the PLANETS whenever he WAS about to lead the ROMAN armies into battle. This is WHY he RELIED so heavily on Egeria the nymph. Not only was she an EXPERT on religious MATTERS, but she also had an ENORMOUS affinity with the ASTROLOgical sciences."

"Guidance," muttered Jim.

"Quaaooo," snorted Brenda.

"Si, she guided Tiberius in many of his DECISions. Many battles were WON because of HER advICE. She became very IMPORTANT to Tiberius the Emperor."

"What eventually happened to her?" Doris asked. "Rark! Is it possible she's still alive?"

Pasqual shook his head, slowly and sadly, and came back to sit in his chair. "Ah, regRETTably, no. Even NYMPHs have their DAY. Towards the end of Tiberius' reign, one CLOUD-filled evening as the legend GOES, Egeria came to the EMPEROR and announced that she was dying. Tiberius was DEVASTATED!

"At first he FORBADE her to die, on pain of DEATH, but then he realised that wasn't GOING to HELP the SITUATION very much at ALL. So he made her FINAL days as COMFORTABLE as he could. After all, Egeria had saved his life, and the lives of his soldiers, inDEED, the LIFE of Roma on many OCCASIONS in the past…

"Just before she died, Egeria asked to see TibERIUS. HE came at once. In a WEAK, whispering voice, she gave him a final GIFT … something that WOULD make his POWER unRIVALLED through the ages…"

"The Bauble?" Doris squawked.

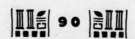

"Not YET the Bauble," answered Pasqual. "Egeria, on her DEATHbed, informed TIBERius that she wished to bequeath to him a VERY special ROCK."

"A rock?" said Jim, confused.

"SI, the very rock upon which ROMULUS and REMUS, the abandoned twin babies, were discovered by the she-wolf who would RAISE them as her own. ROMULUS, of course, beCAME the eventual FOUNDER of Roma in 753 BC."

Brenda swished her tail against the floor, and listened intently.

"EGERIA had known of the whereABOUTS of this special rock all her LIFE, and she TOLD Tiberius that she was saving it for a NOBLE cause. Because TIBERIUS had proved HIMself to be a WISE and STEADY ruler, Egeria decided that it would be HIS."

"But," screeched Doris, "it was just a lump of rock. What's so special about that?"

"AH!" Pasqual clapped his hands together. "It was MUCH more than that, DORis. You see, now that SHE was running OUT of Time, Egeria placed a CHARM on the VERY centre of the Rock of Romulus and Remus. SHE made the EXACT middle CORE of the ROCK *enchanted*." Pasqual leaned forward and whispered – shrilly – to the gathering. "She BLESSED this PART of the rock with the THING that was ELUDING her: TIME ITSELF."

"Well swoggle me with seconds!" gasped Cairo Jim.

"EGERIA told Tiberius that he should EXTRACT

the core of the Rock – a CYLINDER of MARBLE no bigger than his HAND. With this INVALUABLE piece of enchantment in his POSSESSion, TIBERIUS would be able to CONTROL TIME at his WHIM or FANCY. The seconds, minutes, hours, days, weeks – however LONG Tiberius decided – would be at his COMMAND."

"Rark! So he did? And he fashioned the Bauble out of it?"

"Si, Doris. EGERIA told him that this piece of rock would be INDEstructible. It would LAST forever. So Tiberius had his FINEST SCULPTOR fashion the cylinder of rock – cutting it down, down, down until it became very small – into what was to BECOME the IMPERISHABLE Bauble itself!"

Jim shook his head. "I had no idea," he muttered. "I knew the Bauble was supposed to be able to control Time, but I never knew *this* was how it was created. Astonishing!"

"What does the Bauble look like?" thought Brenda.

"What does the Bauble look like?" Doris asked.

"COME with me," said Pasqual, rising and heading for the door. "WE are fortunate to HAVE a bronze REPLICA of the actual Bauble here in the Museum. It is found in the Cosmography ANTEchamber, which is NEVER opened to the PUBLIC."

Jim stood and followed Pasqual. Doris fluttered onto Brenda's fore hump as the Wonder Camel got to her hoofs and went after Jim.

With the aid of a lighted candle, Pasqual led them up the huge staircase once again, their foot- and hoofsteps clacking loudly in the gloom. On the second floor they passed by many rooms and galleries, all of which had a single lighted candle on the floor in the centre of each space.

"Through here," Pasqual said. He paused for an instant and fished out a set of long, thin keys from his trouser pocket. Deftly inserting one of these into the lock of a low door, he gave his wrist a sharp turn. The lock unsnibbed and Pasqual pushed the door open and ducked through the doorway.

Jim followed him, and Brenda (with Doris still on her hump) crouched low and followed Jim.

The walls of the small room were decorated with scenes of maps and countries and other, stranger things: scientific apparatus and astrophysical equipment – weird-looking compasses and spyglasses and measuring instruments – that had been painted in the sixteenth century.

"Here it is," said Pasqual, holding his candle higher so that its flame lit up a small figure mounted on a column in the centre of the antechamber. "An exact REPLICA of the original, which was stolen from another museum in Roma. This replica is THOUGHT to have been made in about the fifth century."

Jim and Brenda came closer to the column, their eyes (and the eyes of Doris) shining with amazement.

Doris caught her breath.

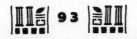

Brenda gave a snort of shock.

The Bauble replica was no bigger than a man's thumb, but it was fierce to behold. It was made in the shape of a lion, perfect to the smallest degree, its jaws opened as wide as they could be, with all of its sharp, minuscule teeth flashing and straining against the gums of the beast. Its eyes were wild and its nostrils dilated. Brenda could not tell if the lion was in agony or was just about to strike at some unsuspecting victim. Its mane was rippling in some unseen wind.

The back of this tiny, frenzied creature was arched and contained a shocking sight: the horns, head and long neck of a goat had erupted through the lion's spine and were sticking straight out of its back. The expression on the goat's face was just as horrible as the lion's.

"TIBERIUS used to wear the Bauble as a PENDANT, on a chain around his NECK."

"Really?" said Jim.

"Si. We know this because there is a STATUE of Tiberius in the VATICAN Museums. He has a rough LIKEness of the Bauble carved ONTO his TOGA."

"Some fashion statement," Doris muttered.

"This Bauble is a SIGHT to behold, do NOT you agREE?"

"It is," said Jim. "For something so small, it's so … so fear-invoking."

"Si. I have a THEORY about that. I think that TIBerius ordered his sculptor to make it as SCARY as he could, so that no ONE would ever CONsider stealing the THING."

"I'd rather have my claws drop off than steal that," said Doris.

Brenda gave her tail a swish against the chilly air in the room, and then she realised something: the lion had no tail at all.

Pasqual explained: "You will ObSERVE that it has NO TAIL. This is BECAUSE the real Bauble does NOT have a TAIL either. Apparently, the tail was made in the form of a SHARP-toothed SERPENT, an angry SNAKE about to STRIKE at the HORNS of the goat."

"What happened to the original Bauble's tail?" enquired Jim.

"LOST," said Pasqual. "Lost in antiquity. Like SO MANY things…"

"If you ask *me*," Doris chipped in, "it's just as well the thing *hasn't* got its tail. It's quite awful enough without any added extras."

"You SQUAWK such a truth, Doris."

The macaw jerked herself up and down, as she often did whenever something was niggling at her. "Pasqual, I'm bamboozled. I just can't see what all this fuss is about. Rark! For goodness' sake, all that's been happening is a series of minor upsets … newspaper vendors selling the wrong papers, people bumping into things, bus tyres going down. What's the big deal? It's hardly catastrophic! Even if the theft of the Bauble is part of this, why should we worry about it so much?"

Professor Pasqual deLirio straightened, his long spine becoming taut and his height towering in the flickering candle flame. He closed his eyes:

"Because, Doris, there is the very distinct possibility that...

"All of the Calamities of Lost History May Be Brought Back to Ruin Us!"

he intoned gravely.

URGENCY REVEALED

JIM WAS SHAKEN by Pasqual's sudden, agitated outburst.

Doris blinked rapidly, and Brenda's humps had tingled with a great zing of foreboding.

Pasqual opened his eyes. "You SEE," he said, his voice still low but rising erratically, "it is all to do with the missing tail. It is INDEED fortunate that the tail is lost, for, if the Bauble were to be reunited with it, then all portents of DISASTER could occur."

Jim ran his thumbnail around his chin. "What do you mean, Pasqual?"

"Ah! I am ABOUT to tell you what only a HANDful of Professors know, someTHING that we have SWORN NEVER to divulge. BUT, because of the present circumSTANCES, and because you, Jim, Doris and BRENDA are involved, I am prepared to BREAK my vow.

"This is the STATE of things: up until now, whomEVER has stolen the BAUBLE has only been ABLE to stop Time for a few SHORT minutes. We know this because, as you SAY, Doris, the things that have been occurring in the afterNOONS have only been MINOR upsets. Small incidents that have

been ANNOYING at one extreme and potentially DANGEROUS at the other."

Doris nodded.

"At PRESENT, seconds of Time are disappearing, VANISHING, being SWALLOWED up. But IF the THIEF were able to FIND the tail of the Imperishable Bauble, and REUNITE that tail with the Bauble itself, then the POWER of the Bauble would be INCREASED hugely!"

Jim could sense his skin being invaded by a battalion of goosebumps.

Pasqual licked his lips and whispered: "If the Bauble finds its TAIL, then not only can TIME be STOPPED, but whoever HOLDS the BAUBLE can REACH BACK into TIME – into the VERY PAST, with all its secrets and neglected knowledge – and UNLEASH whatever FURIES are contained there!"

"Quaaaooooo," snorted Brenda, her tail quivering.

"So much," whispered Jim, his eyes wide with the dreadfulness of what Pasqual was implying. "So much could come back… "

"Si," said Pasqual. "So many horrors, such an IMMENSITY of DIRE power."

Jim's blood chilled. "To think," he reflected slowly, "that such a small piece of ornamentation could become a *tyrannical* emblem!"

"It's almost incomprehensible," Doris screeched.

"Yet it is THUS. My THEORY is that the thief is only experimenting at the MOMENT. He is UNABLE

to do any MORE than stop the SECONDS, and perform minor acts of IRRITATION, because he does NOT have the TAIL."

"And," said Jim, "the tail is lost."

Pasqual nodded. With his index finger he swept the short hairs of his moustache out to the sides. "No one knows where it is. SomeWHERE along the line, it became SEPARATED from the back END of the Bauble and disappeared. But this THIEF is looking for it – I am SURE this is the case, for the THIEF obviously KNOWS that the Bauble can distort TIME, and not many PEOPLE are AWARE of this fact. We had better hope to the heavens that WE find the tail first!"

Jim looked at the replica of the Bauble. "You're right. We either find the tail, or nip the thief in the bud."

Doris shuddered. "I don't want to nip any thief's bud, thank you very much."

"Figure of speech, my dear."

"The tail would be so tiny," Brenda thought, "that it would be like trying to find a single needle in a haystack the size of Africa."

"The tail would be so tiny—" began Jim.

"Si. It would be quite HOPELESS to try to find it, many PEOPLE think. But I have never been one of those people. No, my FRIENDS. In fact, it is because of the missing TAIL that I decided, after I had reTIRED, to come and take ROOMS here in the Palazzo Altemps. You see, this is a very special place. There is a BELIEF that nymphs such as EGERIA never COMPLETELY leave these realms. Oh, si, they may DIE, like we EVENTUALLY will, but someTHING of them remains."

Jim raised his eyebrows, waiting for more.

"But that is another STORY I must tell you, and I FEAR that now is not the BEST time for you all to hear it. I have told you too much, in such a short time, already. One thing I learned from my career: never OVERLOAD the minds of the STUDENTS with too much INFORmation at ONE sitting."

"I can take it," Doris protested. "Tell us, please!"

"I WILL, Doris, but not tonight. Come, let us return to my ROOMS. I am sure you need some rest after YOUR JOURNEY, and we WANT to be FRESH for our important OBSERVATIONS this afternoon, si?"

"Yes," agreed Jim. "We don't want to miss a thing."

As Pasqual led them back to his apartment, he took a huge sniff of the rosy, heavy air. "I shall settle the THREE of you and then I must do my NIGHTLY rounds. I fear that this SMELL might be MEANING that some of the statuary is deteriorATING, and we don't WANT that, do we?"

"No," said Jim. "We've lost enough from the past already." As he descended the staircase with Doris, Brenda and Pasqual, his mind filled with the image of the small tail of the Imperishable Bauble of Tiberius.

And a feeling of helpless dread swept through his legs and stomach.

𝖦 𝖦 𝖦 𝖦 𝖦 **14** 𝖦 𝖦 𝖦 𝖦 𝖦

ROMAN HORRORDAY

AT PRECISELY ONE O'CLOCK the next afternoon, Rome was in the midst of its usual middle-of-the-day bustle. Cars, buses and thousands of Vespa motor scooters roared along the streets and avenues, and the footpaths were thick with Romans and tourists.

By the famous Trevi Fountain, at the Palazzo Poli, hundreds of people were throwing coins into the fountain and crowding onto the terraces, enjoying the sunshine and chattering loudly.

On one of the higher terraces, Cairo Jim and Pasqual deLirio stood, silent and waiting. The eyes of Professor deLirio darted nervously back and forth, from left to right, and the palms of his hands were moist with anxiety.

Beside him, Jim was similarly anxious. He was concentrating on being ready to glimpse any sort of oddness – any person acting strangely, or holding something tiny and precious in an unusually furtive manner. He was concentrating so hard that, despite all the sounds from the tourists around him and the splashing and gurgling of the fountain, he could clearly hear his own heart beating earnestly against his ribs.

"Any little SIGN," Pasqual said in a squeal-whisper. "AnyONE who you might THINK is acting suspiciously, Jim."

"My eyes are more open than they've ever been," Jim murmured back.

"If you SEE such a person, you must KEEP your eyes on him. Do not DARE to look away. For remember, the seconds of TIME which follow will DISAPPEAR and, when Time resumes its normal COURSE, that person will – I have no doubt about this – no LONGER be THERE."

Jim nodded and tilted his pith helmet back from his forehead.

"What WILL remain," Pasqual finished, "is the CHAOS!"

Down on the Via dei Fori Imperiali, outside the entrance gates to the ruins of the ancient Forum Romana, Doris perched on the front of Brenda's saddle.

The Wonder Camel was facing south-east, her snout towards the Colosseum a few blocks away. Doris was reversed on the saddle, her beak westwards, so she could see all the way down the other end of the street as far as the Monument to Victor Emmanuel II (an enormous white building which resembles a typewriter, and is called that by many Romans).

Much traffic coursed down the street, and many tourists were getting off their buses and gathering at the gates of the Forum. Some of the tourists stopped

to take photos of Brenda and Doris, and one man from Austria even slipped a 2000 lire note under the straps around Brenda's chin after he had taken her picture.

(Brenda had snorted with surprise – no stranger had ever slipped her money before.)

"Rerk," rerked Doris with a visible shudder. "These crowds! I'm glad I'm with you, Bren. You and your huge calmness. If I were on my own with all these tourists around me, I'd've taken off long ago."

"Quaaaaaaoooooo," snorted Brenda, rocking her wide neck.

Doris squinted at a clock, high up in one of the Typewriter's towers. "One-thirteen. I wonder if we'll be in the right place at the right time today?"

Brenda kept watching.

Ten minutes passed, with the dragging slowness that time takes when you are waiting patiently for something to happen, but you don't know exactly *when* that something will happen.

More tourists alighted from a big green bus, and a large woman and an even larger man – both in matching floral shorts and striped shirts – came over to Doris and Brenda. The man quickly snapped a photo of the woman, who posed next to them.

"I never knew Rome was so *exotic*," gushed the woman in a loud voice. "The brochures never said anything about these sweeties!" She reached out to tousle Doris's feathers.

"SCREEEEEEAAAAAAAAAAARRRRRKKKKK!"
screeched the macaw, and the woman jumped backwards.

"C'mon, Martha," said the man, swiftly shepherding
the woman into the queue to enter the Forum ruins.

"The cheek," Doris squawked. "What'd she think
I was? A hand towel?"

"The tourists can be a problem," Brenda thought,
"but at least the money they spend on entrance fees
and souvenirs and guide books helps to maintain the
ancient places…"

"Still," Doris muttered, flexing up and down as her
indignation started to subside, "the tourists *can* be a
problem, but I s'pose the money they spend on entrance
fees to places like this and on souvenirs and guide books
helps to maintain these ancient places…"

"Quaaaooo."

Doris gave a small flap of her wings and stared up at
the Typewriter clock again. "One twenty-seven … and
still nothing to report."

From clocks in towers all around the city – some very
old and cobwebbed, others shining and modern – came
the deep, slow tolling of the hour of two.

At twenty-three minutes past two, in the Piazza di
Spagna, near the towering Spanish Steps, nothing
seemed out of the ordinary.

People were climbing the steps, or sitting on
them, drinking coffees or iced drinks. Tourists were

photographing their friends standing halfway up the stairs or halfway down.

Then...

...the afternoon became strangely quiet.

The cacophony of car and bike engines, exhaust pipes and horns; the squeal of tyres on cobblestones and gravel; the sounds of laughter, shouting and loud, enthusiastic talking; the music drifting out of some of the restaurants and cafés and bars nearby – all became muffled, as if an invisible blanket had been slowly lowered over this section of Rome.

And then it was as if the invisible blanket had been straightaway lifted, pulled up with lightning speed, and all the noises and sounds returned, the volume of everything rising back, up and up, louder and louder to its normal, boisterous level.

Then came the ping-pong balls!

From the outside of the church at the top of the Spanish Steps, hundreds of thousands of pure white ping-pong balls suddenly cascaded out of the back of a truck – a truck that nobody had seen arrive; that one second was not there, and the next second was!

Down onto the steps crashed the balls, one after the other, then dozens after dozens, then hundreds, then thousands, bouncing wildly and with great velocity, their high, hollow clattering smacking louder and louder until the din was nearly deafening.

PAKTA-PAKTA-PAKTA-PAKTA-PAKTA-PAKTA-PAKTA!

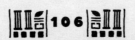

Ping-pong balls followed ping-pong balls like mighty waves surging from the sea, pouring down the steps, bouncing and jumping and speeding wildly.

They bounced off people's heads, they leapt high into the sky, they kept on coming, shooting off at crazy angles all over the place!

People sitting on the steps were engulfed in the torrent. Grown men were pushed off their feet as the swell kept coming and the clattering got louder. People who opened their mouths to scream, or whose jaws dropped with flabbergastedness, found themselves with ping-pong balls wedged firmly between their teeth.

PAKTA-PAKTA-PAKTA-PAKTA-PAKTA-PAKTA-PAKTA!

Ping-pong balls plunged into coffee cups, into baby carriages and prams, into baskets of shopping. Two young lovers had one ping-pong ball break their kiss. Ping-pong balls bounced across the steps, forever downwards, lobbing onto people's faces, on their backs, down their dresses. People slipped and were carried far down the steps by the tide.

PAKTA-PAKTA-PAKTA-PAKTA-PAKTA-PAKTA-PAKTA!

Some people tried to outrun the avalanche, but the ping-pong balls engulfed them, burying them in a few seconds and carrying them down to the bottom of the steps, where they emerged, dazed and discombobulated.

Still the ping-pong balls came, in groups of a hundred here and a thousand there, leaping over the tubs of bright pink azaleas, clattering, bouncing, shooting out in all directions as they hurtled down those stairs.

PAKTA-PAKTA-PAKTA-PAKTA-PAKTA-PAKTA-PAKTA!

Everyone was screaming or shouting to each other or swatting ping-pong balls away as though they were flies.

Finally, after five wild minutes of spherical, bouncing anarchy, the tide had exhausted. The last ping-pong ball bounced slowly down to the bottom of the Spanish Steps.

And everyone was dishevelled and confused.

"Strange," said Cairo Jim, three-quarters of a kilometre south of the Spanish Steps and looking at his Cutterscrog Old Timers Archaeological Timepiece on his wrist.

"What is strange?" Pasqual asked. "Have you SEEN something?"

"No, no. It's just that my watch has slowed. It's never slowed before. It's a Cutterscrog."

Pasqual frowned. "Has it stopped?"

Jim shook his head. He took off his sun-spectacles and examined the watch dial more closely. "Only slowed. And ... well swoggle me silly! It's gaining time again. Look, the second hand's picking up speed."

Pasqual swallowed. "From THIS, I know TWO things. First: some more of the Bauble's TIME-stopping has just taken PLACE. Second: it has not taken place HERE at the Trevi Fountain, because if it HAD, your watch and mine would have stopped COMPLETELY.

This ALWAYS happens after such a Bauble INCIDENT, but only to the WATCHES that were in the immediate AREA."

Jim put his sun-spectacles back on. "Where in Rome was it *this* time?"

"We will find out, my friend. The newsPAPERS will have the story by this EVENING, you can count on it. COME, let us find Doris and Brenda and head BACK to the Altemps Museum."

From out of the Caffé Greco, near the base of the Spanish Steps, a man in alarmingly bright and mismatched clothing stepped into the harsh glare of the pandemonium-filled afternoon.

His small dark eyes surveyed the crowds getting to their feet as streams of ping-pong balls poured off them. On top of his coriander-coloured fez, perched on the knot of the fez's burgundy-coloured tassel, a raven also watched the scene with her throbbing red eyes aglow.

Neptune Flannelbottom Bone pulled down his emerald-green waistcoat and took a long puff on his Belch of Brouhaha cigar. "Arrrrr," he arrrrred quietly.

"Looks like we've found it," croaked Desdemona. She pecked a flea from her wing and spat it savagely into the gutter.

"We've found the *place*," Bone said. He pulled out his gold fob-watch and looked at the dial. "Blast. The thing's stopped, stone-dead."

"Then we *have* found it," Desdemona gurgled. "Watches and clocks always stop when the Bauble's been used. Said so in the papers."

"Watches and clocks always stop when *you* look at them, you unashamed umbra of ugliness."

"Crark."

Bone put the fob-watch away again. "Yes, we have found the place. Now all we have to do is find the *Bauble holder*. And then turn mere mischief – such as what is happening here – into ambitious anarchy of the highest order!"

He hitched up his Crimplene plus-fours trousers. "Oh, how sweet it shall be, Desdemona, to have the power and the glory and all the frou-frou that goes with it once again! This detestable rubbish heap we call 'the world' had better watch out! *Arrrrrrrrrrrrrrrrrr!*"

Part Two:
LOVE AND HISSES

PERPLEXED

"SWOGGLE ME SPHERICALLY!" exclaimed Cairo Jim, putting down the newspaper that evening. "Ping-pong balls!"

He had just finished reading the account to Doris, Brenda and Pasqual of the afternoon's incident on the Spanish Steps, and his face was a map of perplexity.

"It's barmy, that's what it is!" Doris, perched on the back of the chaise longue next to Jim, was jerking up and down, her wings twitching in a high state of agitation.

"Quaaaaaaaaooo," agreed Brenda, sitting on the carpet next to the chaise.

Pasqual shook his head and lit one of the hotplates on the top of his stove in his small kitchenette. "You SEE? THIS is what we are having every afterNOON. These interrUPTIONS of TIME all around us!"

"There's no doubt about it," said Jim. "This is to do with the Bauble. According to the eyewitness reports in this" – he snapped his hand against the paper on his knee – "one moment the truck wasn't there at the top of the Spanish Steps, and the next second it *was*."

"Letting loose the bouncers," Doris said.

"But why ping-pong balls?" Jim asked. "It all seems so ... so *petty*."

"Rark, you're right there." Doris blinked and clacked her beak. "If the thief had wanted to cause real damage, he would've gone for something a bit more dangerous than ping-pong balls. Like bricks or golf clubs or cooking appliances."

Jim looked at her.

"Well," she said, "you'd certainly know it if a five-speed food processor hit you in the back of the head. Not that it's ever happened to me, of course."

"You're right, my dear."

Brenda closed her long-lashed eyes and a calm thought seeped from out of her brain. "Perhaps this thief doesn't want to cause any major damage. Perhaps it's just mischief that he wants to create."

Pasqual had filled a large saucepan with water. He put the saucepan on the hotplate. "You know something? Perhaps this THIEF doesn't WANT to cause any major damage. Perhaps it's just MISCHIEF that he wants to create."

"Quaaaooo," snorted Brenda.

"Mischief?" Jim scratched his chin and thought about that. "But why go to all that trouble to get up to such shenanigans?"

"Maybe," Brenda thought, "this thief is after some attention."

"Maybe," Doris prerked, "the thief craves some attention!"

"Quaaaooo."

"Si," nodded Pasqual. "That MIGHT be all there IS

to it. He just WANTS to be noticed, or MAYBE he is going to MAKE some POLITICAL point ... like the FACT that the PRICE of EGGS is too high."

"Is it?" Jim asked.

"No, no, no, well ACTUALLY someTIMES it is. FAR too expensive – USUALLY I find so on TUESDAYS and FRIDAYS. I have no IDEA why this is. It is MOST annoying, let me tell YOU, for I ENJOY a nice OMELETTE on Tuesdays and FRIDAYS and—"

"Yes," squawked Doris, waddling across to the far end of the chaise so that she could speak directly to Pasqual in the kitchenette. "That *is* a possibility, that the thief is going to make some kind of point. He might be very angry about something."

"Still," said Jim, "angry or not, it's not right for some person to play with time this way. No one has the right to dominate other human beings like that."

"Or birds," added Doris.

"Or camels," Brenda thought.

"Yes. Or birds or camels," Jim said.

Brenda fluttered her eyelashes at him and flashed her teeth.

"Besides," the archaeologist-poet mused, "we don't know how far this person will go to make a point. Today it was ping-pong balls. But if he's looking for the tail of the Bauble, *and if he finds it*, then we'll have a lot more dire consequences to deal with than ping-pong balls!"

"You are RIGHT, Jim of Cairo. But there is nothing we can do right NOW. Except ... how would everyone

CARE for some SPAGHETTI for dinner? Hot, PIPING Spaghetti alla Carbonara, the speciality of Roma and – if I may SAY so – of PASQUAL deLirio."

Jim smacked his lips. "Sounds goluptious, Pasqual."

"Have you got any Malawian snails?" asked Doris.

"Doris!"

"Only asking," she said, her feathers ruffled.

Brenda gave a snort of eagerness – the spaghetti was definitely to her liking as it would be just like eating worms (a delicacy which she enjoyed so much it almost made her speechful).

"I am SURE you will enjoy this meal." Pasqual smiled as he tied a smart, striped apron around his waist. "Even you, Doris."

"Praaark."

"And THEN, after we have DINED, I shall show you around some of the rooms here in the MUSEUM, and fill you all in on a little of the HISTORY of this reMARKable place."

"And why you came here?" said Doris. "Because of the tail of the Imperishable Bauble and all that?"

Pasqual winked at her and emptied the pasta into the boiling water. "If the HOURS of the night are KIND to us," he told her. "Then I shall tell you."

Darkness had come upon the city of Rome like a soft glove slipping onto an old hand.

Neptune Flannelbottom Bone, under cover of the glovelike gloom, sauntered boldly down the Via Condotti.

Ahead of him, lit by weak-beamed lamps, the Spanish Steps loomed and rose up into the night.

Between his teeth Bone clenched a Belch of Brouhaha cigar. With every second step he took, he puffed and exhaled, and the green tinge of the smoke that came out of his mouth, nostrils and sometimes (when he had done a very deep drawback) even his ears made him look like a bloated steam train.

Above and all around him, Desdemona soared through the blackness, disappearing into its upper echelons until only her throbbing red eyes were visible, and then swooping down, razor-sharp beak first, to slice through the air above her companion's fez.

As they approached the famous steps, she came to perch on his flabby shoulder. "Look, look, look," she croaked, pointing her wing at a shop whose window was filled with big tins that contained more colours of ice-cream than she had ever thought possible.

"What is it, you dunderheaded despot of dimness?"

"Ice-cream!"

Bone's eyes followed the direction of her wing. "Gelato. Arrrr," he arrrred, his voice rippling with the remembrance of such deliciousness.

"I wonder if they've got seaweed flavour?" Desdemona said. "I betcha they do – look, they've got every sort under the sun!"

Bone blew a shaft of smoke out of his nose and, taking the cigar from his mouth, licked his lips slobberingly.

Behind the window, the bright crimson gelato studded with cherries, the swirling patterns of butterscotch and chocolate, of lime and orange, of raisins and sultanas and mango – all of these visions seemed to reach out through the glass and beckon him mercilessly.

"C'mon, my Captain," Desdemona urged him. "Let's break down the door, or smash the window, and grab a few tins. There's no one around. What's stopping us?"

He was about to smile at her suggestion, and was a tad's earlobe away from ordering her to smash the glass with her beak, when a thought came to him. "Arrr, no, Desdemona, not tonight."

"Eh?" She clacked her beak shut, stunned at his answer.

"No, we have far more important things to do this very evening. We are about to climb those steps, to inspect very very closely the scene of this afternoon's ping-pong ball pandemonium. There may be a clue which might help us locate the perpetrator."

"Crark. You disappoint me, you do. Here we are in the middle of Rome and you don't even want to sample some of its world-famous ice-cream. Sheesh!"

"Another time. Besides, I'm watching my waistline."

She eyed his enormous belly, stretching his shirt and his emerald-green waistcoat. "Watching your *coast*line, you mean!"

"You are beneath my contempt," he hissed.

"No I'm not, I'm on top of your shoulder."

"You preposterous pile of patheticness. Come with me, up these stairs. It's a good thing that there's hardly anyone about at this hour."

"No, they're all at home in bed, where any normal person or raven should be."

"But if we *do* happen to come across anybody, just press yourself into the shadows. Remember, I am a fugitive from the law, and you do not have to be a raven of the highest intelligence to realise that it is not my dearest wish in this world to be returning to any bastion of incarceration in the foreseeable time to come."

"No, and you don't want to be goin' back to jail in a hurry, either."

Bone stretched his mouth and shot a column of smoke sideways at her.

When she had finished coughing, she rasped, "Thank you *very* much!"

"Come, and keep your throbbing eyes peeled."

"What for?"

"How should I know? Anything that might look suspicious. Out of the ordinary. Like it doesn't belong."

"I'm perchin' on it right now," she thought. But, not wanting another beakful of his Belch of Brouhaha, she held her tongue and kept her eyes open.

Bone stood on the first step and looked up.

A light dew had settled on the Spanish Steps and on the few remaining ping-pong balls that hadn't been collected when the big clean-up had happened that afternoon. Some of these overlooked balls had been crushed and wedged into the tread of some of the steps; others were in corners, sitting there like white, obese little mice not wanting to attract attention to themselves. A scattering of them was lodged in the branches and flowers of the azalea plants in the enormous tubs that were set onto the middle part of the steps.

Somewhere far above, a stray cat brushed against one of the balls. It bounced loudly down the steps (the ball, not the cat), its echo smashing like a repeating gun shot into the still night.

Pakta-pakta-pakta-pakta-pakta-pakta-pakta!

Desdemona shuddered at the sound.

"Be careful, you clumsy carrion!" winced Bone as her talons dug into his waistcoat.

"Carry on is right," she muttered.

The ball continued to bounce, step by step, down, down, down, echoing louder as it approached.

PAKTA-PAKTA-PAKTA-PAKTA-PAKTA-PAKTA-PAKTA!

"The city of Rome," said Bone, "echoes in the night unlike any other city I have ever visited."

"Yeeeerrrggghhh," moaned the raven.

Finally the ball bounced its last, and came to land at the feet of Bone, vibrating up and down against the point of his shoe as though it had a strange case of the hiccups.

The large, fleshy man lifted his shoe and brought it heavily down onto the ball. "That should put you out of

your mindless misery," he sneered, squashing it flat. Then he took a deep breath, and a deeper inhale on his cigar, and started climbing the steps.

As he puffed on the cigar and ascended the wide, famed steps, his eyes sleered from left to right, trying to detect anything out of the ordinary.

Desdemona's eyeballs, throbbing red and dimly, also tried to spy any clue.

After half a dozen steps, Bone stopped and wiped his sweaty forehead with the back of his hand. "Arrrr, it's no good. It's too dim here."

"Just like you," Desdemona thought, and gave a gurgling snigger.

Bone pulled out a fat candle from the back pocket of his plus-fours trousers. He took a match from his waistcoat pocket and whispered, "Let there be light!"

With a sudden lunge, he scraped the match against Desdemona's tarsometatarsus. The match sprang to life, and fifty-seven fleas were incinerated.

"AAAAAAAAARRRRGGGGGGHHHHHHHH!" howled the bird.

"Enshut yourself! Do you want the police to hear us?"

"Oh, pardon me. I'll just singe here quietly."

"Arrr." He brought the match to the wick of the candle.

"Now," he said, throwing the match away and holding the glowing candle before him, "keep watch!"

Once again he began to ascend the steps, being

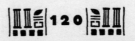

careful not to tread on any lingering ping-pong balls (lest he slide and fall over) or any litter (lest he foul his precious spats).

When he and Desdemona had climbed two dozen steps, he stopped and looked down, surveying the territory they had just covered. There was nothing out of the ordinary anywhere – no objects or graffiti that might have been left by whoever it was who had caused the disturbance earlier that day.

"Maybe," suggested Desdemona, "they might've left a note or a letter or something pinned up on one of them lamp posts?"

Bone held the candle a little higher, and waved it in the direction of the nearest lamp posts. All he could see was the fancy, scrolled iron of the posts, sparkling with the night's dew.

"You mephitic mound of moronic mishmash," he hissed.

"You're very welcome," she rasped back at him.

On he climbed, up and up.

Soon he was grunting, and his thighs were trembling, and his back was awash with sweat. "The truck," he gasped, "appeared up there, to the right. Just beside – erf – that church. That is – ugh – that is the place – ooh – where I am heading."

"Keep goin' big boy, it's about time you had your annual bout of exercise."

"Ugh. Arrrr."

Then Desdemona became agitated. "Scraaaarrrk!"

She flapped a wing against Bone's perspiration-riddled cheek. "Stop! Stop right here!"

"Watch it, you'll have my eye!" He stopped climbing and held the candle up between himself and the raven. "What is it, you startled squib of sick-makingness?"

"Over there." Her voice was low, and she signalled to the left by poking her beak into the gloom.

"Where?"

"There. I seen something in that tub of rozaleas."

Bone looked at the tub of flowers in the centre of the steps. He eyed Desdemona, then looked again at the tub.

"Go on, go on, go on," Desdemona urged.

He padded across the stairs, the sweat on his brow intermingling with the dewy air around him.

When he was right above the tub and the azaleas, he held the candle high. "Where? What?"

"A black thing," she answered hoarsely. "Small. Squarish."

Bone peered through the flowers, and began to part them with an impatient fist.

"It was stickin' up at an angle under the bush," croaked Desdemona. "I'm sure I saw it, when the candle flickered higher for a sec."

Bone stopped trying to part the azaleas. "Well don't just perch there like Canute in a drought," he growled. "Hop down and rummage in the dirt!"

"Me?"

"You!"

"I don't dabble in the dirt! I'm a raven of refinement."

"And I'm Shirley Temple." He clenched his cigar between his teeth, grabbed her by her throatfeathers, and thrust her savagely down under the azalea bush. "Find it, and hurry!"

"SCRAAAAAARKKKKK!"

He stood over her while she scrabbled about in the moist dirt, between the roots and branches. After a minute, she poked out her beak, and her eyes throbbed at him in the dark. "Got it!"

"Give, give, give," he ordered.

"Please, please, please," she retorted.

He lowered his voice until it was full of threatening innuendo. *"Give it to me right this instant, or you will no longer know the meaning of the word 'existence'!"*

She belched and then thrust her beak back under the bush, clamped it around the small, black object that was there, and brought it out into the candlelight.

With a small cough and splutter, she spat the object into Bone's outstretched palm.

His flabby lips curled downwards, the Belch of Brouhaha cigar sticking out of his mouth at a strange angle. "Is this all?" he asked.

"Yep. What'dya expect, the Taj Mahal?"

"A mobile phone," he seethed. "A stupid, blasted mobile telephonic instrument. Why, every idiotic tourist and bank manager and politician has one of these wretched things at their disposal. There are more of

these in the world than there are hot dinners! Arrrrrrr!"

"Maybe it's a clue?" suggested Desdemona.

"Clue my armpit! It's been left here by some sun-dazed tourist who probably doesn't even know they've lost it. Nincompoops of the world unite!" He puffed angrily on his cigar, sending foul shafts of smoke into the night.

"Ah well, toss it away and let's get on with the search. Throw it down there, and break a window if ya can! Hek hek hek!"

"Arrrr." He lifted the phone and was just about to lob it far, when his heavy eyebrows shot up and his expression changed. Slowly he lowered his arm and stared at the phone with a new, keener interest. "Well, heavens to the Goddess Betsy," he whispered.

"What?" Desdemona hop-fluttered out from under the azalea bush and perched on the edge of the tub, looking up at him. "What's come over you all of a sudden?"

"Shhhh!" For a full minute he studied the side of the mobile phone, his caterpillar-like eyebrows rising and lowering, his nostrils dilating widely.

Finally Desdemona had had enough. "Ya gonna share it? Or should I go and lead my life somewhere else?"

"That would be a great blessing for me, but not right now. Look, Desdemona, here, on the side of the phone."

He held it, and the candle, closer to her eyes.

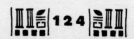

"See? A series of letters has been engraved onto the phone's outer casing!"

Desdemona squinted. Hesitantly (for she was not very good at reading unless there were pictures with the words) she spoke the letters: "W-A-S-P-I-T-S-R-A-M-B. Waspitsramb. WASPITSRAMB?"

"WASPITSRAMB," nodded Bone, a strange look in his eyes.

"What does WASPITSRAMB mean?"

"It means that I think I have found the perpetrator behind this afternoon's – and all the *other* afternoon's – disruptions." Carefully he slid the mobile phone into his waistcoat pocket.

"Really?" She looked at him with slitted, curious eyes.

"Arrrr. And therefore I have discovered who the thief of the Imperishable Bauble of Tiberius is!"

"Who? Who? Who?"

He inhaled the cigar smoke deeply into his lungs and then shot it from his mouth, to blow out the flame of the candle.

"Time, as I have told you on many occasions in the past, will reveal all." He patted his waistcoat pocket. "Or maybe I should say that in *this* instance, the mobile phone shall reveal all."

"Eh?"

"I have a very strong hunch that we will shortly receive a telephone call on this very phone. And that call, my curious crepuscular companion, will lead us

to the person we are searching for. And then to the Bauble itself!"

"Well smother me in treacle and call me a delicacy," muttered Desdemona.

With huge, confident strides, Bone began descending the steps. "Little did I know," he said, his voice rippling with the promise of what he hoped lay ahead, "that tonight would echo with such a discovery! Arrrrrrrrr!"

POST PASTA

"THAT WAS THE BEST SPAGHETTI that's ever journeyed over my taste buds, Pasqual."

Cairo Jim sat back on the chaise longue, his stomach full and his poetry cells springing unexpectedly into action. Before Doris, Brenda or Pasqual could stop him, he was declaiming:

"Is there nothing our Professor
can't succeed at if he tries?
His lectures were terrific,
they brought tears into my eyes,
his cooking is astounding,
in the kitchen he's a master –
I'll not forget, as long as I live,
his Carbonara pasta!"

"Quaaaaooo," agreed Brenda as she slurped the last strand of spaghetti from her plate.

"Ergggghhh," moaned Doris.

"What is the MATTER, Doris?" Pasqual leaned forward in his chair. "Did dinner UPSET you?"

"Rark, no. Not *dinner*." She gave Jim a sideways look, but he didn't notice it – he had his head back against

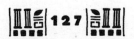

the chaise longue, and was staring up at the ceiling (which was beautifully decorated with a 300-year-old painting of cherubs and palaces and dimmer things that he couldn't recognise).

Doris flew across the room, from the table where she had been eating, to Jim. She swooped down and landed gracefully on his kneecap. "So, Pasqual," she squawked, "will you tell us why you came here to live in this place?"

Jim smiled at the keenness of his small feathered companion.

Pasqual inspected his watch. "Ah, SI, there is time. I shall TELL you." He looked at Doris and laughed. "There is no DOUBT about it, you are a very perSIStent bird when you want to KNOW something, are you NOT?"

Doris blinked at him. "Relentless curiosity is a trait amongst the more intelligent birds, such as macaws. It's natural to us."

Brenda gave a snort, swished her tail against the carpet, and thought, that's for sure!

"That's for sure," Jim said, tousling Doris's crest.

"Rark."

"All right," said Pasqual, settling himself into the deep upholstery of the armchair and looking up at some point in the middle distance of the room that was also far away, far back in his past.

"I retired EARLY from being a lecturer, as you know, Cairo Jim, and I knew at ONCE that I had to come to Roma. You SEE, even though I had spent

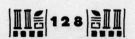

most of my LIFE telling students about the WONDERFUL history of ancient ITALIA, there was an UNANSWERED bit of that history – a mystery from LONG AGO – that I wanted to TRY to solve.

"It all had to do with the missing TAIL of Tiberius' BAUBLE. Now, I have NOT told any of this to a single PERSON, macaw or WONDER CAMEL, but here is the time to divulge it."

Jim, Doris and Brenda listened keenly.

"Shortly before I RETIRED, I attended a special MEETING of the SEPARATE."

"The SEPARATE?" said Jim, looking puzzled.

"Si. The group of Select Emeritus Professors of Ancient Rarities, Artefacts, Treasures and Emily."

"Emily?" said Doris.

"Si. She is the DOG that belongs to one of the other Professors. She ALWAYS comes along to the meetings."

"Ah." Jim still looked puzzled.

"You are ALLOWED to look puzzled, Jim, for it is a highly secretive group. The only people who can become MEMBERS of the SEPARATE are Professors who have proved themselves to be EXTREMELY knowledgeable about an AREA of ancient Roman HISTORY."

"And Emily," Doris added.

"Si, and Emily. ANYWAY, at this meeting, ONE of the Professors – Professor Phyllis Edwards, who is an expert on early TOGAS and ornamental shoulder SASHES from the Late Republic Period – revealed something NEW and ASTONISHING to us all. It was

so AMAZING that even Emily got excited, all over the FLOOR, in fact."

"Yes?" said Jim, his eyebrows raised.

"Yes?" squawked Doris in a 'keep going' sort of voice.

"Quaaaoooo?" snorted Brenda, her neck stretching forward.

"Tell us more," Jim urged.

"Oh, SI. A DREADFUL mess. It took us AGES to clean it up, mainly because no one could find a BUCKET and MOP, and then when someone DID—"

"No," said Jim, "not that bit. Tell us what it was that Professor Phyllis Edwards revealed."

"Ah!" Pasqual clasped his knees. "It was to do with the missing TAIL of the Imperishable Bauble!"

Jim felt his heart beating ever-so-slightly faster.

"Professor Phyllis Edwards DISCOVERED, during one of her regular late-night visits to the University of Tuscania Library, an ancient MANUSCRIPT that had been written by a scholar more than 1600 years ago. Around about the time we believe the TAIL went MISSING from the BAUBLE.

"This manuscript revealed something HITHERTO UNKNOWN by all of the MEMBERS of the SEPARATE group. Something that FINALLY made me decide to LEAVE my academic career, and to COME to live HERE in the Palazzo Altemps MUSEUM."

"What was it?" asked Jim.

Pasqual unclasped his knees and leant forwards. "The manuscript told us that when EGERIA the

nymph gave the rock to the emperor TIBERIUS, she also put a CHARM on an ancient STATUE. This charmed statue was thus ABLE to sing!"

"Well swoggle me with a soprano," gasped Cairo Jim.

"To sing?" crowed Doris.

Brenda's mane started to slowly stand on end.

"Si. To SING. This was not all that UNUSUAL for ancient ROME. I have read of at least HALF A DOZEN ancient statues that were SUPPOSED to have been ABLE to sing to people. Apparently, it used to HAPPEN quite a bit.

"But what made this statue even more SPECIAL than the other singing statues was WHY and WHEN it would sing. The manuscript told us that the STATUE would only SING if the TAIL of the BAUBLE was ever removed from the BAUBLE itself. When that happened, the statue would SING and tell of the WHEREABOUTS of the Bauble's missing TAIL."

"Extraordinary," muttered Jim.

"The statue will sing," said Doris, trying to fully understand it all, "to tell where the missing tail is."

Brenda's mane was so stiff that it looked like some maniac hairdresser had got carried away and put a whole tube of hair gel into it.

"But," continued Pasqual, "only the RIGHT person would hear the statue SING. It would not sing to just ANYBODY. It seemed that EGERIA placed such a CHARM on the statue so that it would IMMEDIATELY recognise the right sort of LISTENER. According to the manuscript discovered by Professor Phyllis Edwards, that LISTENER had to be wise, pure of intentions, and had to have perfect MUSICAL pitch. If a person did NOT possess these THREE qualities, then that person would NOT hear the SINGING, and would not know where the missing TAIL was."

"The statue," Doris half-screeched, "what does it look like? We have to find it, and *fast!*"

"What *did* it look like, you mean, Doris." Pasqual sighed heavily, as though he had a hod of bricks on each shoulder. He stood and went over to his desk.

Opening the drawer, he pulled out an old, yellowing page in a clear plastic sleeve. This he brought back and gave to Jim. Brenda stood and came around behind the chaise longue so that she could also view what was on the yellowing page.

"That was what it looked like," Pasqual told them. "Professor Phyllis Edwards made copies for all of us SEPARATE members."

Jim, Doris and Brenda studied the drawing on the page. It was of a marble statue of a beautiful young woman: tall, with long arms and legs and a slender neck. She was standing with one elbow raised and her hand touching the back of her neck. The other arm was down, and was nestled against her beautifully rounded hip, with her hand concealed behind her lower back.

Around her body was carved a sort of diaphanous piece of material, made out of marble but looking as though it could be the flimsiest and lightest silk garment ever made. Her hair was tied back behind her neck, and her non-eyes – for they were merely egg-shell-like mouldings in her strong, marble face – were staring blankly out from the page.

Her chin was delicate, her nose strong, the marble of her cheeks smooth and flawless.

Her lips, which were full and pale, were parted slightly, as though she were about to open them fully and sing her wonderful song.

"The manuscript said," Pasqual informed them, "that it was RUMOURED that the statue was CARVED in the exact LIKENESS of EGERIA herself."

As Brenda stared at the drawing, her mane began to settle down again, and a strange but not unwelcome tingling started to spread down the inside of her neck and further back, into her humps.

"She's beautiful," Jim said quietly. With the exception of his good friend, Jocelyn Osgood (who was not made of marble but flesh and blood), he had never seen such a striking woman.

"She WAS beautiful."

"*Was?*" Doris blinked. "What happened to her?"

Pasqual went to his armchair and sat down again. "If only we KNEW," he sighed once more. "Like so MANY ancient statues from antiquity, she was LOST, or DESTROYED. Maybe she is buried BENEATH our very FEET, claws and HOOFS. We don't know."

Jim put the page down. "Have people searched for her?" he asked.

"Ah, SI. Everyone in the SEPARATE group has done huge SEARCHES through the records of museums and art GALLERIES and private collections. EVERY man, woman and their DOG has searched. Even Emily has had a go."

"And what do you think happened to her?" Jim smiled at his erstwhile Professor.

"Ah! Well now, THAT is what has led me here. This museum is a PECULIAR place, my friends. A VERY peculiar place indeed..."

PASQUAL EXPLAINS
THE PALAZZO

PASQUAL STOOD AND LIT a candle. Then he went to the door. "Come, per favore, and I will show you ALL what is so SPECIAL about the museum."

Doris hop-fluttered up onto Jim's shoulder, and the archaeologist-poet stood and followed Pasqual, who had left the apartment and was heading up the monumental staircase.

Brenda went after her friends, silently and watchfully. Her humps still tingled with that strange sensation, but it was not unpleasant, and she let it continue, enjoying the mystery of it.

As Pasqual led them up the stairs he told them, "This palace – for that was what it was, before it was turned into a MUSEUM – was started some time before 1477 and was completed after 1568 by the Cardinal Marco Sittico ALTEMPS. Cardinal Altemps was a man who LOVED to collect ancient STATUES and SCULPTURES and artworks from LONG AGO."

"A man of great taste," said Jim, his Sahara boots echoing dully on the steps.

"SI," agreed Pasqual. "Sixteen of the STATUES in the museum date BACK to Altemps's original COLLECTION. This original collection was broken up

after Altemps's death, and sold to MANY different people. Most of the REST of what you will SEE in the museum is from the collection of ANOTHER Cardinal, Ludovico Ludovisi."

"Ludovico Ludovisi," repeated Doris. "Cooo."

"Ludovisi," said Pasqual, "was a nephew of Pope Gregory XV, so as you can IMAGINE, he was very WEALTHY. This was GOOD for him, because he, too, LOVED to collect ancient artworks. In those days, STATUES from ancient ROMA were being dug up EVERYwhere and ALL the time. Ludovisi was ABLE to buy WHATEVER he wanted."

They had climbed two flights of stairs and now proceeded along the southern loggia – a long verandah with a high, vaulted ceiling. A series of doors led off it.

"We're going to the Cupboard Room," Pasqual said, "so called because on the far WALL you will see an old PAINTING of a cupboard with wedding GIFTS laid out on it. COME, follow me."

They followed him into the Cupboard Room, which was very spacious and high-ceilinged. On the floor in the centre of the room was a small round bowl with a big white candle burning in it.

"That bowl," Pasqual said, "I put in here this afternoon, before the SUN began to disappear. I do this EVERY night, in EACH of the rooms here in the Palazzo. It is part of my HOPEFUL search."

Jim looked at him, but said nothing.

There were three enormous white marble statues

flickering in the light from the candle. Pasqual went over to one of these statues and held his own candle high so that everyone could view it without too much flickering.

Then he spoke, quietly and (for once) in a very calm voice:

"When Cardinal Ludovisi was buying all his statues, unfortunately most of them were in a damaged state. This was because the excavators were in such a hurry to get the statues out of the ground – the quicker they could unearth statues, the quicker they could make money. So many beautiful and fine pieces were damaged so stupidly because of the GREED of the excavators and the buyers."

"Quaaaooo," snorted Brenda sadly.

"Si, Brenda, it was not good. But Ludovisi brought all the pieces of all the statues back here and then he employed some of the greatest sculptors and artists of his day to restore them. To put them BACK TOGETHER. And, when pieces of the original statues were MISSING, these sculptors and artists would CREATE NEW pieces to replace them."

"Rark!" Doris jerked up and down on Jim's shoulder. "That explains it!"

"Explains what, my dear?" Jim asked.

"Well," she squawked, "that first night when we came here, Brenda and I were peering in through all the open doorways while Pasqual was taking us to his apartment. And it occurred to both of us that something about these statues that we were seeing didn't quite look right."

"You are very ASTUTE," Pasqual said, smiling at her.

Brenda swished her tail but snorted nothing.

"Even though," continued Pasqual, "Ludovisi employed the finest artisans of his day – people like Bernini and Buzzi and Algardi – to repair the artworks, their efforts are quite OBVIOUS. Many times the COLOUR of the NEW marble does not match the colour of the ORIGINAL marble. And other times, the artists could only IMAGINE what might have once been sculpted. They had to use their imaginations to COMPLETE the statues."

"So what you're saying," Jim offered, "is that many of the statues and sculptures here in the museum probably bear no resemblance to how they would have originally looked?"

"EXACTLY," nodded Pasqual. "Sometimes, the artists even ADDED new bits to the sculptures. Take this particular statue, for example." He lifted his candle higher. "This is an ancient Roman copy of an original Hellenistic-age statue. It is Ares, the Greek God of War."

"I thought he looked familiar," Doris chirped.

"See how he SITS next to his huge round shield, ready to draw his SWORD? Well, look CAREfully. The handle of the sword features the head of a demon, SI?"

"Yes," observed Jim.

"Rark."

"Quaaaooo."

"Well that part is an ADDITION, carved there in 1622 by Gian Lorenzo Bernini, who restored the statue."

Cairo Jim bent and looked carefully. "Yes, it's a different type of marble altogether."

"And," Pasqual said, "look at Ares' nose."

Doris fluttered up and onto Pasqual's shoulder. "Rerk, I can see the joins where his nose has been attached to his face!"

Brenda squinted at his neck. "And the head," she thought. "The head's from a completely different statue. There – there's where it's been joined to the torso."

"Si," Pasqual said. "You will also notice that the HEAD is from a completely DIFFERENT statue." He ran the candle flame around the shoulders and the upper body of Ares. "Here are the points where it has been joined to the torso."

Jim gasped. "Even those four fingers are from somewhere else."

"From Bernini's own hands," said Pasqual.

"Yergh," shuddered Doris.

"No, my dear," Jim soothed, "Pasqual means Bernini carved them from marble with his own hands."

Doris blinked. "I knew that."

Pasqual pointed out the small marble baby with wings on its back that was snuggled behind Ares' right leg. "That cherub is also an addition, although I THINK Bernini took if from the REMAINS of another ancient statue and put it down there."

Jim was astounded as he perused Ares and kept noticing more and more pieces of the statue that didn't seem to have belonged to the original: the right foot, the left ear, the top, rounded section of the shield … even the small knob of his outstretched wrist. "It's like … an ancient jigsaw puzzle that Bernini put back together," he said.

"Si, using pieces from many other ancient jigsaw puzzles to finish this one."

Doris flew off Pasqual's shoulder and all around the statue, checking out the back as well.

"Ares is TYPICAL," Pasqual said, "of so many of the pieces in the Palazzo Altemps Museum. Hardly ANYTHING in here is complete. There is even one statue of a Roman senator, on the ground floor, that is over FOUR METRES tall. It was reconstructed just from the original NOSE!"

A gentle swell of realisation washed through Jim's body. "And now I understand," he said to Pasqual. "Now I think I know why you came to live here."

Pasqual smiled at his former student. "You tell me why, Jim of Cairo. You always were a bright and quick learner."

"After that meeting of the SEPARATE," Jim began, "you became intrigued with the idea of the singing statue. Am I right?"

"Si. Correcto."

"And you knew that it had been lost, most probably destroyed or smashed into many – possibly *hundreds* – of pieces."

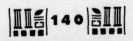

"Si, you are on the right track."

Doris landed on Brenda's head, between her ears. She and the Wonder Camel listened intently.

"And you knew of the Palazzo Altemps, and how there's not another museum like it in the world, where so many of its statues had been put together again and remade from so many different ancient fragments?"

"Si again."

"So you came here, to live here full-time, in the hope that maybe ... just *maybe* ... there was the remote possibility that a small part from the original singing statue that Egeria the nymph put a charm on might be somewhere in this place? *Somewhere on one of these many statues?*"

Pasqual clicked his long fingers. "Spot on, Jim!"

"Well I'll be grounded!" Doris screeched.

"Every night," Pasqual told them, his voice rippling with optimism that knows no bounds, "I light my candles in every room in this place. Every night I wander the halls and galleries in the hope that some small part of one of these statues might sing its secret song ... and lead me to the TAIL!"

He went to the other side of the room and sat on a wooden bench that was against the wall. "I have made it my quest, if you like, to try and hear the singing statue, or rather any LITTLE PIECE that might have come from the original singing statue. And, if I were LUCKY enough to hear it, I would be able to get the TAIL and put it somewhere where it would NEVER be able to be reUNITED with the Bauble!"

Jim came and sat next to him.

"But," Pasqual whispered, his lower lip trembling, "so far, no good. I have heard not a NOTE, not a WARBLE, not a TUNE or MELODY in all my thousands of nights on patrol here. The only sound has been my footsteps, passing from room to room."

There was nothing Jim, Doris or Brenda could say, squawk or snort. The feeling of helplessness in the air was heavy; almost as heavy as the statues around them.

"And now," Pasqual said, his eyes moist and his voice wavering, "the time has come when we need to hear the singing. NOW more than ever!"

On the other side of Rome, in a lavish suite at the Hotel Forum, a mobile phone rang, sharply and shrilly.

A pudgy hand put down a gold-plated manicure stick (which had been stolen in its zhooshy case that afternoon) and placed a fat cigar into an ashtray. The hand picked up the phone and pressed a button.

Then Neptune Bone raised the phone to his hairy ear. "Hello?" he whispered.

Perched on the end of the four-poster bed, Desdemona watched him as he listened to a voice. She saw his eyebrows creep slowly up his wide and glistening forehead.

"Crark! Who is it? What're they sayin'?"

Bone moved the phone away from his ear and put his

other hand over it. He sneered at Desdemona, "They asked for Cairo Jim!"

The raven's eyes throbbed hatefully at the sound of Jim's name. "Goody-gumbum! Mr Wholesome! Cairo Manners-Maketh-the-Man Jim! Why? Why are they asking for him?"

"Be quiet, and I'll play along." He put the phone back to his ear, and spoke in a higher and more flattish sort of voice. "Yes, as a matter of fact, this *is* Cairo Jim speaking. How did you know it would be me?"

Desdemona watched as he kept listening.

"All right," he said, "let's meet then. I'd love to see you again! Oh, yes. Yes indeed! I look forward to it. Okeydokey then, wonderful, wonderful. At midnight tonight? Yes, yes. The Forum Romana. Yes, it's very close. And you'll tell me everything. Good-o! See you then. Cheerio!"

He rang off and threw the phone onto the table.

"Oh," Desdemona croaked, "I think I'm gonna be sick! To hear such jolliness and genteelities come outta your chubby chops! Yeerrrrrgggghhhhh!"

Bone sat back in his armchair and began to laugh, silently, heavily, his many chins quivering beneath his beard, and his belly wobbling under his opened waistcoat.

"Anyway," the raven asked, "who was it? Dja know 'em?"

Bone's laughter grew and multiplied, and found its way to his throat. Great bursts of sound erupted, and his eyes brimmed with tears. Soon there were waterfalls of tears, splashing down into his beard and moustache.

"Oh, I was right, all right! HAAARRRRR HAAARRRRRRR HAAAARRRRR HAAAAAAAAA-RRRRRRRRRRRRRRRR!"

MIDNIGHT

FOR THE NEXT FEW HOURS, Pasqual gave Jim, Doris and Brenda a guided tour through the Palazzo Altemps Museum.

He showed them many rare and beautiful statues and sculpted objects which, as he had told them earlier, had nearly all been reconstructed from many other ancient statues and sculpted objects.

He led his friends through dozens of rooms with high, vaulted ceilings and walls which had been painted similarly to the wall in the Cupboard Room, hundreds of years ago.

They inspected the monumental, multi-coloured marble fireplaces, with statuary and carvings and busts of long-dead cardinals set high into the tops of the fireplaces.

They went into the opulent church of Sant'Aniceto, a private church that was housed on the top floor of the Museum. Here Pasqual showed them the resting place of the remains of one of the first Roman popes, Saint Anicetus.

They walked the corridors, grand corridors with marble columns and stairways that seemed to have been in existence forever. The echoes of their foot- and hoofsteps lingered long after they had gone.

Nowhere did they hear a single note from any portion of Egeria's ancient singing statue.

At about half past eleven, Doris saw a small sculpture, and she knew at once it was her favourite. It was of a head – there was no body, or even much of a neck attached to it. It was the head of a young man or woman (it was impossible to tell which) and it was resting on its cheek on a dark green marble slab. The eyes were closed, and it looked so peaceful, so restful, so full of sleep, that Doris opened her beak and had a long, gaping yawn.

Jim saw her and he, too, yawned.

Pasqual did likewise.

Only Brenda, who slept very little on account of her natural Wonder Camel metabolism, didn't yawn. Instead she snorted – a soft, I-think-it's-time-for-bed-for-all-of-you type of snort.

Jim stretched his arms and back. "Goodness," he half-yawned again, "all this walking and travelling and everything seems to have caught up with me. I'm weary."

"You can yawn that again," Doris said.

"Si. Maybe we should retire for the night. We shall want to be alert for TOMORROW, si? Maybe that will be the day when we shall be in the right PLACE to witness whatever disruptions of TIME will most definitely occur..."

"Rark. Grand idea, Pasqual."

Without another word, he led them back to his rooms.

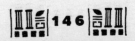

★ ★ ★

The ruined columns of the Forum Romana loomed out of the thick blackness of the night like a tableau of enormous sepulchral candles waiting to be lit.

Tonight the midnight-moon was almost full, and it bathed the closed and deserted grounds in a wash of glimmer that was nearly bright enough to cast shadows. A few cats wandered about the columns, their tails snaking around the old, weathered marble and disappearing into the unlit gloom behind.

"Oh, great," croaked Desdemona, peering from Bone's shoulder through the padlocked iron gates that blocked their access to the grounds. "Cats! I need cats like I need a flea circus!"

"They shall do you no harm, you wary waste of woefulness. Here, make yourself useful. Hop down and whack open that padlock with that beak of yours."

"Can't you pick it with a bobby-pin or something?" she whined.

"What, and risk chipping one of my recently manicured fingernails? Don't be ridiculous!" He grabbed her by her skullfeathers and thrust her down to the lock.

In this vice-like grip, she knew there was no escaping. With three savage whacks of her sturdy beak, the padlock came apart and dangled limply from the gate.

"Arrrr. You see, even *you* have your uses."

"Yeah, and when there's a worldwide shortage of bloatedness, you'll be in demand as well," she muttered indistinctly.

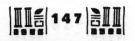

Bone's ears were not open to such sounds at the moment – he was relishing his anticipation of the meeting which was soon to take place. He reached down and pulled the padlock away, tossing it onto a nearby grassy verge, where it landed with a dull thump.

With a haughty arm he shoved open the gate and strode boldly down the path, into the Forum Romana. Desdemona flew close by.

"Arrr," he breathed heavily, "just think, Desdemona. Thousands of years ago, the ancient Romans moved through these streets, living their pathetic little lives and conducting their drivelling little transactions…"

"Crark!"

"The armies of the Caesars marched through that great archway down there as they left for another war to win eternal glory for the Roman Empire…"

"Crerk!"

"And now, here, tonight, I, Neptune Flannelbottom Bone, am going to obtain an item of such rare value that this ancient Forum will be the launching place for *my* sashay into the world global domination racket! So great will be *my* power that I shall put the memory of the ancient Roman military efforts into the dustbin of History! Arrrrrrr!"

Desdemona looked at him and belched loudly.

"You obnoxious orb of odiousness. You'll be belching on the other side of your beak one of these days."

"Yeah, yeah, yeah."

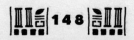

"Enough of this banter. You will fly for me, Desdemona, fly all over these grounds and see if you can spot another human being. And be quick – there is a heavy dew settling on and inside my plus-fours, and you know how I detest becoming clammy."

"It's a little late for that," she thought, pecking at a flea. "You were *born* clammy and, unlike the Roman Empire, some things *never* change!"

"Well, what are you waiting for?" He lunged out, grabbed her by her left leg, and hurled her far up into the night.

"Scraaaaaarkkkk!" she wailed as she helplessly somersaulted through the air. Then her velocity slowed and she regained control.

Bone watched the black outline of her wings as she soared upwards and then across the sky above him. Fleetingly her silhouette flitted against the moon; at other moments she was merely a smudge scudding silently through the dimness.

"Come on, come on," the fleshy man murmured. "Seek, seek seek!"

Back and forth she flew across the moonlit ruins.

Somewhere a cat miaowed, the sound drawn out and terrible, almost as if it were being pulled from the cat's throat by a pair of pliers.

"Hurry," snarled Bone, squirming and shifting on his feet as the clamminess started to sink into his double watermelon posterior regions.

Then there was a whoop-whoop-whoop of feathers,

and Desdemona swooped down to land on a fence railing not far from Bone's elbow.

"This place is creepy," she croaked, pecking quickly at a coterie of fleas on her belly.

"Well? Did you see anyone?"

"Crark. I think so."

"You *think* so? You have never been known to indulge in *that* activity."

"Let me put it this way." She glared at him, her red eyes throbbing angrily in the dark. "I am under the impression, based on my own first-talon observations during my recent reconnoitre of the specific region, that there is indeed a human presence in the ruins of the Forum Romana. I detected such a presence between the third and fourth columns of the Temple of Saturn, approaching from the west. I hope the Captain finds this information useful and acceptable."

Bone's eyes lit up, firstly because she had seen someone, and secondly because of her display of language. "You pretentious pile of pong," he sneered. "You sound like you've just been concussed by a dictionary."

"You should talk. That's like the pot calling the kettle Kevin."

"Imbecile." He started walking down the ancient Via Sacra, towards the Temple of Saturn. His footsteps crunched loudly on the gravel.

"Scraark, wait for me! I don't wanna be left alone with all these mangy cats!" Desdemona lifted her wings and shot away to fly closely behind him.

"Nearly there," whispered Bone as he passed the bare foundations of the Basilica Aemilia, once the centre for money and finance dealings more than two thousand years ago.

The Triumphal Arch of Septimus Severus loomed large in front of them, shining white and square in the night. Bone stopped for a second and stared up at the arch.

"Arrrr," he arrrred as he imagined how very soon, if his plan went according to his wishes, there would be the grandest procession in his honour passing through this very monument.

"The Temple of Saturn's over to the left," croaked the raven in his ear. "Down that path, behind them bushes."

"I know my way around this site," he hissed at her. "I *am* a fully trained archaeologist, remember!"

"Crark."

He turned on his heel and strode down the smaller path, being careful not to prickle his stockings against the coarse, twiggy branches of the small bushes that lined the sides.

All eight columns of the Temple of Saturn appeared, suddenly and silently. This, and the partly ruined pediment above them, was all that remained of the once magnificent building.

Bone stopped, and Desdemona swept down to land on his fez. The large, clammy man strained to peer into the darkness.

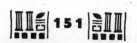

For several seconds he looked, trying to find any evidence of another person.

Finally he rolled his eyes upwards at the bird. "So this is where you reckon you saw someone?" he asked dubiously.

Her eyes throbbed hard as she scanned the darkness by the columns. "There was someone there, sittin' between those two columns, right in front of us! I'm certified!"

"You *will* be one of these—"

A rustling of the dry grasses behind the Temple stopped him. Bone and Desdemona held their breaths and waited.

The grasses rustled again. Then, from the other side of the Temple, a figure climbed the steps and slowly emerged into view.

Desdemona's beak dropped open. "I ... I ... I know who that is," she stammered.

"Of course we do," Bone said, his beard bristling. "As soon as I heard the voice on the mobile telephone, I knew my deduction was right!"

Now the figure stood above them. "You are not Jim of Cairo," the woman said, frowning.

Bone removed his fez and raven. "Indeed, I am not, madam," he answered, half-bowing to her. "There has been a slight complication..."

MEMORIES ARE
MADE OF THIS

BRENDA THE WONDER CAMEL was sitting next to her saddle on the mat in the corner of Pasqual's living room, her legs folded beneath her and her eyes open and watchful.

On the other side of the room, Jim was stretched out on the chaise longue with a dark blue blanket covering him. He had fallen asleep almost as soon as he had lain down, and now his slumber was a deep one, filled with images of the Imperishable Bauble of Tiberius and its missing, snake-headed tail (which appeared in his dream as big as a house, instead of being smaller than a pinkie finger), as well as his good friend, Jocelyn Osgood (who flew into his dream every now and again and smiled warmly at him and then flew away again), and another event: seeing himself winning the International Poetry Championships in Baden-Baden, Germany.

Somehow, Brenda was able to see, in a gauzy, half-lit sort of way, what he was dreaming on this particular night. Her heart did a cha-cha-cha when he dreamt about the International Poetry Championships part.

Doris was also asleep, perched on the edge of a wooden lectern that Pasqual had found in another room

and had set up just for the macaw. Her head was tucked under her wing, and Brenda could see her little heart beating gently against the yellow feathers on her chest.

And Pasqual was dead to the world in his bed in his bedroom. Through the opened door, Brenda could hear an occasional soft and gentlemanly snore, ruffling the stillness.

The Wonder Camel gave a small snort and flicked her tail against the mat. Try as she might, she couldn't sleep. This didn't surprise her – being the type of Bactrian she was, she needed very little sleep. Most of her nights were spent thinking and remembering and being as calm as the still desert sands when not a whisper of wind is blowing.

The apartment was quiet, just like the whole of the Palazzo Altemps Museum. Just before midnight, before all the clocks in all the rooms had chimed, Brenda had heard a mouse scrabbling. The noise of its claws was so amplified against the marble and the emptiness, it sounded like a miniature army marching through the place.

Then, after the last of the clocks had struck midnight, and the miniature mouse battalion noises had died to nothing, Brenda's ears stood up, alert.

In a place far away, but close enough to be near to her as well, she had been called!

Brenda blinked and shook her head. Something had sounded her name.

BRENNNNNNNNNNDDDDDDDaaaaaaaaa.

Once.

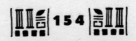

Almost piercingly sharp at the beginning.

But gentle at the end.

Brenda's highly developed Wonder Camel hearing enabled her to pick up sounds far too high for humans or macaws or other creatures to discern.

BRENNNNNNNNNNDDDDDDDaaaaaaaaa, she had heard.

She closed her eyes and tried to think what the sound could have been. Was it just that she was very tired, and perhaps she'd imagined it? Strange things had happened to her in the past when she was on the brink of exhaustion.

She thought far into herself and judged the amount of energy that was still stored in her humps. No, she decided. She was hardly tired at all. It wasn't that.

Had it been a sound from outside? A tree branch scratching against one of the windows, for example, and its sound carrying through the Museum in a high-pitched wail?

Something told her it wasn't that – the calling she had heard was not a scratchy sound, but was mellifluous as well as being sharp. A tree branch against glass would not have been like that.

Slowly, the hairs in Brenda's mane began to creep up. She felt them stray from the back of her neck and rise stiffly and uncertainly.

Brenda opened her eyes. She sensed what was to happen next.

BRENNNNNNNNNNDDDDDDDaaaaaaaaa…

This time it was higher, and it sounded as though it was beckoning.

Beckoning her.

Making as little noise as possible, Brenda got to her hoofs and stood. Quietly she tip-hoofed to the closed front door of the apartment. Using her dexterous teeth, she turned the doorknob and eased open the door.

Then, as if she were as light as a butterfly, she began climbing the stairs.

As she went higher, she sensed the way, although she did not hear her name being called.

When she got to the second floor, she turned left and walked through a loggia, the walls of which were painted with scenes of cherubs and angels and dark, ivy-covered forests. On each side of the loggia, set onto short pedestals all along the floor, were twelve head-and-shoulder busts of all the ancient emperors of Rome, who were known as the Caesars.

Brenda moved amongst them, looking out of the corners of her eyes at their pale white faces and their see-nothing-see-all eyes.

At the western end of the loggia she found two things: a beautiful fountain set against the wall, decorated with sculpted women carrying water jugs and three cherubic fauns playing in a big clam shell and, right at the top, a pair of aquatic goats with spiral fishtails, just like the Zodiac sign of Capricorn. Next to the fountain was an open doorway.

Here she stopped and listened.

A tiny breeze wafted through the loggia, rushing around Brenda's kneecaps and then onwards, where it swirled silently down the stairs.

Brenda's mane still stood on end, and her humps were beginning to tingle – a sensation that she could well do without right at the moment.

Then, just when the tingling was on the rise, the calling came again…

BRENNNNNNNNNNDDDDDDDaaaaaaaaa…

Now it was louder, and the Wonder Camel knew that it was coming from one of the rooms on the other side of that opened doorway.

She took a deep breath, raised her head and neck high, and went through the door.

Pasqual's candles in their bowls were still burning in the centre of the floor in each room she wandered through. Her hoofs clacked on the wooden floor of the small church of Sant'Aniceto as she travelled quickly to the galleries on the other side.

The first gallery was huge and square, with an enormous marble fireplace in it, adorned with carved animals and a crest and two beautiful women caryatids who held up the mantlepiece with their creamy white hands. It was the fanciest fireplace Brenda had ever seen.

Brenda continued to the next gallery. This room was smaller, and all it had in it was an ancient sarcophagus, and some marble reliefs attached to the walls.

Brenda paused in this room. She looked all around.

She listened hard, without any distractions clouding her frequency range.

BRENNNNNNNNNDDDDDDDDDAAAAAAAA…

This time it was louder than it had been so far, and – Brenda was sure of it – it had come from just around the corner!

She flared her nostrils and realised that her eyelashes were moist with perspiration. With a brave swish of her tail, she slowly left this room and entered the next.

She felt hesitant, but not altogether scared, when she came into this room. The first thing she noticed was the walls. They had been decorated with fragments of frescoes, each of which featured an obelisk in the centre. Because Brenda had seen lots of *real* obelisks back in Egypt and on her and Jim's and Doris's travels to many other countries, and because obelisks were her favourite sort of ancient architecture, she felt a calming, soothing sensation almost straight away. It was a bit like being greeted by an old friend she hadn't seen for some time.

She gave an agreeable snort, and looked around the rest of the room.

On four big square bases there were four bigger-than-lifesize statues. Even in the glimmer of the candle flame in the centre of the room, Brenda could tell that all of the statues were fragmented, and had been cobbled together from many other marble sculptures.

She lumbered closer to the first statue to have a better look. It was of a male nymph sitting on a rock with a man who had two horns sticking out of his head and the lower body of a goat. The nymph was obviously annoyed at the satyr – Brenda could tell from the look on the nymph's face and from the way he was elbowing the satyr in the ribs.

The statue next to it was of Pan – who looked very much like the satyr – and Daphne. Brenda recognised the couple from a book of Greek mythology that Cairo Jim had read to her and Doris back at their camp in the Valley of the Kings. She gave a quiet snort as she observed that Daphne was annoyed, too. That would have accounted for the way she was slapping Pan on the head.

Brenda let her eyes flick over the many different colours of marble contained in both statues: pink, green, creamy white, pure white, faint brown and even a peachy hue here and there. How many original pieces of sculpture, she wondered, did these statues come from?

She turned and, without taking a step, she found herself snout to pedestal with the third statue in the room. A small bronze plaque was fixed to the pedestal, and Brenda read the writing on the plaque:

DADOPHORUS
THE TORCHBEARER
ROMAN COPY OF AN ORIGINAL GREEK STATUE
(WITH ADDITIONAL BITS AND PIECES ALSO)

She looked up at the white and cream and greenish figure that was standing above her. It was a youth, completely naked, who, in his left hand, bore a burning

branch above his head, carved out of yellow-coloured marble.

His stomach was clearly an add-on, for Brenda could detect a line that circled the abdomen, joining this section of the sculpture to the hips. The abdomen was a different colour to the hips and the upper legs.

The right arm of the Torchbearer was different, too ... there had been some cosmetic surgery done near the elbow and the wrist.

The curls on his head were more frenzied than one would expect on an ancient statue.

Then Brenda's heart skipped a beat!

She was moving her gaze down the Torchbearer's face, past the smooth forehead and the obviously added-on, straight nose, when she came to his lips. These were full and round – Brenda could tell at once that they were a bit too big for the original face. They also had a strange blue tinge, a colour Brenda had not seen before.

Around the lips, at the very edges where they joined the Torchbearer's marble cheeks and the area above his chin, were the unmistakable marks of a sculptor's chisel.

Brenda's humps went cold, very quickly. Then they went warm, just as fast, and then cold again.

A low, soft stirring began deep within her.

She stood before the Torchbearer, her breath hardly coming out of her nostrils, her eyes transfixed by the lips of the statue.

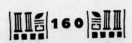

The Wonder Camel could not move a muscle, or bristle a hair in her tail.

And then it came, as deep down she sensed it would:

The statue remained frozen, locked in time. Every inch of him remained completely still. Every inch except the three inches where his lips sat incongruously on his face.

Slowly, with no sound at all, the lips changed colour.

The blueness in them melted, and was soon replaced by a glow of soft pink.

And, when all the marble in the lips was this new, pink colour, the lips parted.

Brenda's heart was pounding, but she could not snort. She had never in her life been so amazed.

The statue kept staring beyond his lit torch. He did not look at Brenda. Separately from the rest of him, the lips on his face continued to part, until they were smiling.

Pasqual's description of the hearer of the singing statue whooshed around Brenda's mind: "the LISTENER had to be wise, pure of intentions, and had to have perfect MUSICAL pitch. If a person did NOT possess these THREE qualities, then that person would NOT hear the SINGING…"

Brenda had no idea whether she had perfect musical pitch. She was soon to find out.

The lips on the Torchbearer's face closed. When they opened again, a voice came from behind them – a voice as mellifluous and as sweet as the purest honey.

A voice that was high, beautiful, eyelash-curling and spine-shifting. A voice that was all these things, yet urgent as well.

The voice that had called her name, that only she could hear.

And it *sang*:

"The minute thou walked in the joint—"
("Quaaooo quaaooo," snorted Brenda.)
"—I could tell thou were a camel distinctive,
the quiet Brenda.
Soft-snorting, so refined,
able to communicate with only thy mind..."
("Quaaaaaaoooo!")
"So let me sing right to the point—"
("Quaaoo quaaoo!")
"—I don't sing out loud to every Bactrian:
listen, Brenda ...
the tail is in the Pantheon!"

The high, urgent song stopped and, as Brenda watched, the lips of the singing statue closed again and changed colour, fading back to the light blue they had originally been.

For many minutes Brenda stood, staring at those lips. The lips from the statue of Egeria. But they didn't move again.

Gradually, the Wonder Camel's heartbeat returned to its regular rhythm, and her pulse slowed, and her

mane and eyelashes relaxed again. She shook her head and swished her tail as her mind set out on its next course.

The Pantheon, she thought.

She knew, from her accidental but fortunate exposure to encyclopaedias and certain architecture magazines when she was a very small calf, what the Pantheon was. More importantly, she knew *where* it was, here in the middle of Rome.

All she needed was the map that she had left in her saddlebags, back in Pasqual's apartment. That would help guide her through the narrow and confusing streets.

Something inside her was telling her that she should fetch that map, and waste no time in getting to the Pantheon. There was trouble afoot out there – she didn't know exactly what, but she could sense it as a Wonder Camel can sense such things – and she knew that there was no time to waste.

She had to find that tail tonight.

A DEAL IS STRUCK

"YEAH," CROAKED DESDEMONA hoarsely, "we've met that dame before!"

Neptune Bone beheld the petite young woman with the lustrous dark hair standing at the top of the steps of the Temple of Saturn. Her deep brown eyes bored down into the large, fleshy man with a blaze of anger.

"Captain Bone," she said, her voice soft but seething. "We meet again."

"Meltem Bottnoff," Bone said, bowing slightly. "As I knew it would be."

"Eh?" said Desdemona. "Howdja know it'd be her?"

"My phone," answered Meltem Bottnoff.

"Arrr." Bone withdrew it from the back pocket of his plus-fours. "I read the letters engraved on it. WASPITSRAMB. I knew at once it was yours."

Desdemona hopped onto the top of a broken column. "WASPITSRAMB? WHATSITMEAN?"

"Tell him, Captain."

Bone sighed. "Listen carefully, you dim dab of dumbness. The letters stand for: Worldwide Antiquities Squad Phone, Istanbul Turkey. Senior Retriever of Ancientness Meltem Bottnoff."

"Craaark."

Bone addressed Meltem Bottnoff. "I do think, madam, that it was very careless of you to leave it there, for anyone to stumble across."

At this, her eyes lit up. She threw back her head and laughed into the night.

It was not the laugh of a young woman enjoying a joke or a stupid remark, but something far more cruel, far more savage.

The feathers along Desdemona's spine hackled at the sound. "She's weird," she muttered to Bone.

He said nothing, but listened as Meltem Bottnoff's laughter came to a sharp stop. She rushed down three of the stairs and then halted suddenly, glaring at him and the raven.

"Careless?" she said, her voice a mixture of a hiss and a singsong lilting. "You think it was careless of me to leave the phone there? You really think I left it there by *accident*?"

A trickle of sweat emerged on Bone's forehead and began to run down it. The manner of this woman was unnerving him.

"Well," he answered, attempting to sound as natural as possible, "I assumed—"

Her eyes penetrated him like two diamond-pointed drills entering a slab of cheese. "When you *assume*, Captain Bone, you make an *ass* out of *you* and *me*!" She kept her eyes fixed firmly on him, and laughed loudly and wildly once again.

"Very droll, madam," Bone remarked.

Her laughter stopped immediately. "I did not accidentally leave my phone on the Spanish Steps, in that tub of azaleas! I planted it there!"

"That's a bit stupid," muttered Desdemona. "Planting something like *that* in there. It's one thing for the azaleas to grow in that dirt, but a mobile phone? I mean ta croak—"

"She means she placed it there deliberately," Bone said. "So that we would find it."

"No!" Meltem shouted, scuttling down the last five steps until she was standing before Bone and the raven. "Not so that *you* would find it. So that *he* would find it, and come to find *me*!"

"He?" said Desdemona.

"Jim," explained Bone. "Jim of Cairo."

"Jim of Cairo," Meltem repeated in her singsong voice, and a faraway look crept across her eyes.

"But why?" Bone asked, taking a small step backwards.

"He stole something from me," she said, her eyes snapping back to Bone.

"Cairo Jim? *Stole* from you?" Bone could scarcely believe it.

"Well I'll be plucked and basted," gasped Desdemona.

Meltem Bottnoff nodded. "Back in Turkey. You remember the time we had in Turkey, don't you, Captain Bone? When Jim and Doris and Brenda the Camel of Wonder and myself tried to stop you from exploiting the power of the Great Goddess Artemis and Her Legendary Petticoat?"

"Arrrr," he arrrred, his beard bristling at the memory.

"Back in the days when I was still working as a Senior Retriever of Ancientness for the Antiquities Squad."

"You mean," Bone asked, "that you no *longer* work for that dreadful organisation?"

"I quit," Meltem answered. She raised her delicate chin in a gesture of defiance. "There was no longer a place there for me. Not since my encounter with Cairo Jim."

"Arrr." Bone took a Belch of Brouhaha from his pocket and quickly lit it. He exhaled the foul smoke with the attitude of a man who has just discovered that he holds the upper hand. "So now it seems, madam, that we are on the same side of that wretched regulatory system we call 'the law'."

"The same side?" said Meltem in her strange lilt.

"Oh, yes." He thrust the mobile phone at her. "When you left the Antiquities Squad, you *stole* this telephonic instrument, yes? Why else would you have it when you no longer work for that deluded organisation?"

Meltem said nothing.

Desdemona listened intently, not even aware of the chomping fleas in her wings.

"But," continued Bone, "that is not *all* you have purloined, is it? I bet my bottom lira that somewhere, in one of those pockets in your lime-green blazer or your chic brown corduroy slacks, you have secreted a tiny, ancient object."

Still, Meltem was silent. She looked at him with her wild eyes.

"A tiny, ancient object," he growled, "known to the moronic masses as the Imperishable Bauble of Tiberius. Oh, it makes perfect sense that you have it, madam." He puffed a column of smoke up through his moustache, past his fez and into the dewy night. "With all the knowledge that you would have gleaned from working for the Antiquities Squad for ... how many years was it?"

"Ten," said Meltem. "Ten long years and five long months."

"With all the knowledge you would have obtained during that time, you would surely be aware of the powers of the Bauble, not to mention at which museum it was kept here in Roma."

She lowered her chin and looked at him severely. "Of course I took the Bauble, you grossly inflated egotist!"

"Arrr," he said, shuddering slightly at her outburst.

She reached into a pocket in her blazer. When she withdrew her hand, her small fist was curled around something. "I knew that if I had this, and if I used its powers to distort time and create havoc, then Cairo Jim would be here to investigate. It was the only way I knew to get him to come."

Bone's heart started beating very quickly at the thought of the object in her fist. "Show me, show me, show me," he murmured.

"Behold, Captain Bone, the Imperishable Bauble of Tiberius!"

Slowly Meltem uncurled her fingers. There in her upturned palm, bathed in the strong moonlight, lay the tiny, agonised lion-and-goat Bauble.

"Bad things *do* come in small packages," croaked Desdemona.

"Once worn around the neck of the emperor Tiberius himself," Meltem said. "Made from the very rock that Egeria the nymph had described, the rock upon which Romulus and Remus were discovered as abandoned babies."

"Hey nonny-nonny and a ha-cha-chaaarrr!" exclaimed Neptune Flannelbottom Bone, his great hide ablaze with goosebumps.

"And this I have been using to stop the seconds of Time. To create situations that would entice Jim to Rome." She looked strangely at the Bauble. "I did not want to cause major catastrophes, only minor annoyances. Things that would disrupt, rather than destroy. Things that would surely capture the attention of the archaeologist-poet."

Bone listened to her, and in his heart he despised her. Why not go all the way, he thought, why not cause huge, terrible calamities, when such power is at one's fingertips?

"That is why all the occurrences have been merely annoying," Meltem said. "Letting tyres down on buses, swapping newspapers, changing the clothes and shoes that people are wearing. The worst thing was the ping-pong balls. I did not want to hurt anyone, just disturb the course of things."

"You have a long way to go, madam, in the evil department." Bone took a long drag on the cigar, then smiled in what he imagined was a pleasant expression. "I wonder if you would be so kind as to give us a brief demonstration of how the Bauble actually works?"

Meltem looked at him, then at the raven, then at him again. Then she held the Bauble to her lips and uttered some words into it.

Neither Bone nor Desdemona could understand the words, but Bone could detect that they were Latin.

Bone waited.

Desdemona waited.

It seemed that nothing had changed.

"Well?" asked the fleshy man. "Will you or won't you?"

"I have," said Meltem.

"What?"

"I have just used the Bauble, as you asked. I stopped Time for thirty seconds."

"Ha!" sneered Bone. "And I'm a nun's wimple!"

"Craaaarrrk!" squawked Desdemona. "Look, look, look at me!"

Bone spun around on his chubby heel. Desdemona was still perched on the broken column, but now she was wearing Bone's fez.

Bone's hand shot up to his greasy curls. "Heavens to the Goddess Betsy," he gasped. "It works!"

"Of course," Meltem said.

He went to put the cigar into his mouth, but there

was a sudden, hissing singeing of his moustache, and the smell of burning whiskers filled the air.

"AAAAAAAARRRRRRRRRR!" he wailed, patting down his facial hair.

"Yes," Meltem advised him, "be careful. I about-turned your cigar as well."

When Bone's hairs were extinguished, he snatched the fez back from the raven and plonked it onto his head. "Very impressive," he seethed.

"It could be so much more impressive, for someone like you," said Meltem, "if I had the tail of the Bauble as well. With that attached, there is much more that could be accomplished."

"The tail?" questioned Bone.

"Yes, Captain Bone. Surely you, with your archaeological knowledge, know of the relationship the tail is supposed to have with the Bauble?"

Bone thought for a moment, but he had no idea about the tail of the Bauble. Being the man he was, however, he did not intend to reveal his ignorance. "Oh, *that* tail. Of course. Arrrr."

Meltem pressed the Bauble close to her chest. "I plan to begin searching in earnest for the tail tomorrow," she said. "My efforts so far have not lured Jim here. It is time, I think, to start getting a bit more serious. Time to let everyone know that I mean *business!*"

"Pray enlighten us, madam, just what the tail could do. I, of course, know, but my raven is more than a tad uneducated, and information is always a welcome guest to the threshold of her underprivileged skull."

"You'll keep, you fancypants garbage heap," muttered Desdemona under her seaweedy breath.

"I'll do better than that," Meltem told him. "Come, I'll *show* you."

She walked past him, and disappeared down the path that led to the Arch of Septimus Severus.

"Come, bird," ordered Bone, clicking his moist thumb and forefinger. Desdemona flew onto his shoulder and they followed her.

They found Meltem standing under the colossal Arch, a tiny figure dwarfed by the magnitude of the marble all around and above her.

"Listen," she said urgently. "I have come here on some nights when I can think of nothing other than Cairo Jim and what he has done to me. On those nights I have pushed the power of the Imperishable Bauble as far as it will go while it has no tail. Watch and listen. This is a taste of what *could* be…"

She held the Bauble close to her lips again, and uttered into it.

Standing in front of the Arch, Bone watched the diminutive woman.

Desdemona's eyes throbbed redly.

The dew settled heavily around them as they waited.

Then Bone's spine stiffened, and the raven shot off his shoulder and into the air!

Underneath him, the ground shifted as though it was a mat being pulled slowly away!

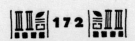

"What in the name of Richter?" began Bone.

The ground continued to shift and shudder beneath his feet. He had to stand with his legs apart to keep his balance.

"Craaarrrrk!" wailed Desdemona, flying about near his head. "Listen! Whatsat?"

As the ground moved this way and that, a noise seemed to be erupting from beneath it. A deep, jangling, blaring noise, dull and discordant.

It rose up through the earth, up into Bone's feet and all the way further as it travelled through his body. He slammed his hands over his ears, trying to repel the awful noise.

"It's a … sounds like … some sort of trumpets!" he cried. "Thousands of them! Arrrr, turn it off, madam, I beseech you!"

The ground was now moving like an ocean being tossed by a hurricane. Back and forth Bone stumbled, into holes that began to open up, and then out of them before they closed again.

The blaring of the subterranean trumpets – if that is what they were – increased. Bone pressed his hands as hard as he could against his ears, but it was no use: the din was coursing through his body.

"PLEASE," he screamed as great torrents of sweat poured from him, "STOP THIS! I AM A MAN OF GREAT SENSITIVITY, AND I—"

Meltem took the Bauble away from her lips, and put it back into her pocket.

As quickly as it had started, the commotion stopped.

"What you have just witnessed," Meltem said, "is a foretaste of what could be possible if I were to reunite the tail with the Bauble. Once that happens, I will not only have the power to stop Time for brief periods as I can now, but I will also be able to reach back into History ... to bring back the Time that is trapped from so long ago."

"You mean...?"

"Yes, Captain. I will be able to *superimpose ancient Time onto modern Time*. And I will bring back whatever I want from the ancient past, into our world. This way I will be able to achieve my goal!"

She threw her head back and laughed so shrilly that the fleas in Desdemona's feathers went on a major biting binge.

"And your goal is the getting of Cairo Jim?" asked Bone, dabbing at his sweat-pouring forehead with a handkerchief.

"Exactly! I had hoped that by this time, I would have lured him here. I had hoped that I would have no need to go after the tail. I had expected that he would have come by now."

Bone listened.

"But it has not worked," Meltem said. "Cairo Jim has not come. All I have got is *you*!" She started breathing strangely, faster and faster, and her eyes grew wilder and bigger, their dark brownness deepening by the second. "Therefore, I now have no choice

but to find the tail, and let Time do its worst! With the *full force* of the Bauble at my fingertips, Jim *has* to meet me!"

"My Captain," Desdemona whispered at Bone, "she's gettin' weirder!"

Bone raised his hand, pretending to rub his nose. In a stabbing hiss, he whispered back, "This is a woman who, for one reason or the other, has been tipped over the edge. We must be very careful with her."

"Nevermore, nevermore, nevermore," spouted the bird.

Bone lowered his hand and, in the next instant, it seemed to him that all of Fortune had somersaulted into his lap. He realised that he had some knowledge that Meltem did not. His lips spread into a flabby smile, and his caterpillarian eyebrows wiggled.

"Madam," he purred, "if I were to tell you that Cairo Jim were procurable, would you do a trade with me?"

Meltem stopped her strange breathing, and looked far into his beady, manipulative eyes. "What do you mean?"

"I mean, I happen to know that Jim and his awful entourage are here in Rome at present. They visited me a few days ago in Cairo and told me they were coming here, to try and sort out the business of the Bauble."

"Really? You are not lying to me?" She pointed a delicate finger threateningly at his chest. "For if you *are*—"

"No, no, no, I assure you I speak the truth! Let me make you an offer: if I can obtain Cairo Jim for you, would you give me the Bauble?"

A stillness came over Meltem's body. She went and sat on a granite plinth, near the entrance to the Arch of Septimus Severus. "If you deliver Jim to me by this time tomorrow, you can have the Bauble," she said. "I very much want that Jim of Cairo."

There was something in her voice, and a strange, new fire in her eyes, that made even Neptune Bone shudder.

"Consider it done," he said. "By half an hour after midnight tomorrow, we shall have brought him to you. Come, Desdemona, we have work to do."

Meltem looked up into the sky. The moon filled her eyes. In a thin, lost voice, she started to sing: "The night is bitter…"

Bone had taken a few steps, when he turned back to Meltem. "By the way, madam. You told me that Cairo Jim stole something from you. Exactly *what* did he steal?"

Meltem stopped singing. She spoke softly. "Such questions you ask. Such answers will come when you have fulfilled your end of the bargain." She looked back into the sky, and sang again: "Stars have lost their glitter…"

"Arrrr," said Bone, before striding purposefully away into the gloom.

THE NIGHT THICKENS

THE PANTHEON, Brenda recalled – from the dark night several years ago when, not being able to see what she was eating, she had accidentally consumed volume nine of the *Encyclopaedia Britannica* in her home oasis – is one of the most beautiful ancient buildings in all of Rome.

As she walked slowly and carefully through the narrow streets with their rough cobblestones underhoof, she remembered the words she had eaten:

"Restored during Hadrian's reign, from AD 118 to 125, the original building was built by Agrippa between 27 and 25 BC. The monumental building originally honoured all the gods of ancient Rome. Inside, statues and busts of all the gods were placed on altars around the circular walls. The great dome, with a hole (or oculus) in the top to allow the sun to shine in, was the biggest dome of its time and represented the heavens. The Pantheon and its dome still stand intact, and today it is lined with the elaborate tombs and sarcophaguses which contain the remains of Italian kings and artists."

A small shudder passed through her humps when she remembered the last bit, but Brenda gave a snort of resilience and continued onwards.

Her hoofs CLACKED loudly on the cobblestones. The CLACKing smacked back off the buildings on either side of the street, and echoed hugely all around the neighbourhood.

CLACK-ta-CLACK-ta-CLACK-ta-CLACK-ta-CLACK!

There was no one about as she made her way through the weaving streets and dimly lit alleys. Every now and then she would stop under a street light (when she could find one) and consult her map. Then she would look up at the stars, decide where north was, inspect the map again, and continue on her way.

Her memory filled with the picture of the Pantheon that had been printed on the encyclopaedia pages she had swallowed. (Being a Wonder Camel, the words and illustrations had remained in her subconscious, forming an enduring personal library and photographic database inside her head.) As she lumbered along, she saw the image behind her eyes at the same time as she saw the street in front of her.

A beautiful building, its dome rising far up towards the skies, with a grand portico in front of it made up of dozens of tall, strong columns.

Here, Brenda knew, she must search with every iota of her intelligence and cunning.

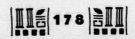

As the image grew in her mind and behind her eyes, she continued through the alleyways and streets, her hoofs echoing like sombre drumbeats into the lonely city.

CLACK-ta-CLACK-ta-CLACK-ta-CLACK-ta-CLACK!

Cairo Jim rolled over on the chaise longue. In a tangle of blankets and cushion and his gaberdine extra-wide Sahara shorts, he tumbled onto the floor of Pasqual deLirio's apartment.

"Oof," he grunted, rubbing his arm. He picked himself up and sat on the chaise longue again. With a yawn, he stretched his arms wide and squinted at his Cutterscrog Old Timers Archaeological Timepiece.

There was just enough light in the room to see that it was a few minutes after 1.00 a.m. Like a pig's tail, he thought. Twirly. He said the word out loud and smiled.

He turned on the small lamp on the table at the end of the chaise. Over in the corner he could see Doris, deeply asleep on her lectern. Her beak and most of her head were tucked under her left wing, and Jim couldn't see any of the light green feathers that adorned the top of her head. Her chest-plumage rose and fell as she took in and exhaled tiny breaths.

He smiled again and swivelled around, to the corner where Brenda had her sleeping mat. And his smile vanished.

"Brenda?" he whispered, standing and going to the mat. "My lovely?"

He crouched and frowned at the empty space. Then he stood and tiptoed to the opened doorway.

"Brenda?" he called quietly up the staircase.

No answering snort came back.

His heartbeat quickened, for he knew that it was not like her to go wandering off in the middle of the night. As a young calf she had often wandered away, usually to play with other young camels, but she hadn't done it for years. Something must have disturbed her to have made her get up and go elsewhere.

He padded over to the lectern and gently rubbed the back of Doris's neck. "Doris? My dear? Wake up."

"Rarerark." The macaw raised her head and opened her small eyes. She blinked at Jim's gloomy silhouette as he stood between her and the opened door. "Jim?"

"It's me."

"What's the fuss?" She could tell from the way he had said those last two words that something wasn't quite right.

"It's Brenda. She's not here."

Doris raised both wings and stretched them. "Where is she?"

"I don't know. We should find her, though – I don't want her wandering around by herself. Not while Rome's at the mercy of the Bauble holder."

"Right." She jerked up and down on the lectern. "We're better off together under the present circumstances."

Jim held out his arm and Doris stepped off the

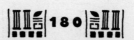

lectern and onto his wrist. With a few quick hops, and being careful to keep her wings close to her body, she was up onto Jim's shoulder in one second.

"Her saddle's still there in the corner," she observed.

"Let's go and search the Museum," Jim whispered. "We won't wake Professor deLirio until we have to. Maybe she's up in one of the galleries somewhere."

"I'll fly up and have a search," cooed Doris. "I can cover all the rooms on wing faster than you can on foot."

"Good idea, my dear. You fly up to the second floor. Scour all the rooms there. I'll follow in your tracks."

He put on his pith helmet, and sniffed loudly as the smell of roses and kerosene filled the apartment. He looked confused.

"See you upstairs, then," Doris said quickly. She raised her wings and fluttered off through the door.

Jim followed. By the time he got to the foot of the staircase, he saw her small shadow disappear through the arched doorway at the top of the stairs on the second floor.

For the next ten minutes, with skilled swoops and turns, Doris flitted through the rooms and corridors and galleries.

"Bren?" she called out, not loudly, but urgently. It was as if she were reluctant to screech too raucously and disturb all the statues during this still hour.

Many of the candles in the bowls on the floors had almost burnt to nothing by now, and there was not very much light in some of the places she flew around. But there was still enough illumination from the remaining candles, and from the strong moonbeams shimmering in through the tall, unshuttered windows, for Doris to have detected her friend's large and noble shape.

She saw no such shape anywhere.

Jim wandered through the rooms in Doris's wake. "Brenda? My lovely? If you're playing hide-and-seek, we give up! Come out if you're here!"

No snorts greeted him.

No sounds of any sort came from any of the rooms.

Doris appeared through the doorway ahead and swooped in to perch on the end of a bench. "No trace at all," she announced, blinking worriedly. "Not even the trace of a trace of her."

"Apart from the statues, the place is empty," said Jim, his voice hollow with uncertainty.

"Like 'an empty casket, where the jewel of life by some ... hand was robb'd and ta'en away'," Doris quoted from Shakespeare's *King John*.

Jim gulped, then shook his head. "Let's not get our feathers in a fluster without good reason, my dear. Let's put ourselves in her hoofs. Maybe she's ... maybe she's just gone down to the ground floor?"

"Rark! Yes! To stretch her legs or something. I'm off at once!" With no more ado, Doris flew for the door leading to the stairs.

"I'll follow," Jim called out after her. "As soon as I've finished up here..."

What made him stay for that extra bit longer up there

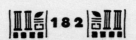

on the second floor, he couldn't say; but something, somewhere, deep inside him, was telling him to walk back to the staircase the long way.

Through all of the rooms on that floor.

Slowly.

He wandered through the galleries, going the opposite way to the way he had come. As he passed the pale and frozen marble figures, something began to throb in his temples.

It grew louder with every room he entered. By the time he came to the obelisk room, he could feel the sides of his forehead pounding.

The archaeologist-poet took a deep breath. He had no idea why his head was carrying on like this. He put out a hand to steady himself.

His hand touched the base of a statue. Jim's forehead was pounding wildly by now. He took his hand away from the marble and looked up at the Torchbearer.

For some reason, Cairo Jim's gaze was immediately drawn not to the Torchbearer's upstretched arm, nor to his curls, nor to his eyeless eyes, but to his lips.

His closed, locked lips.

Jim stared at the lips, noticing the colour: the gentle light blueness of the marble.

Slowly, the pounding in Jim's head subsided. In half a minute, he could feel it no more.

He watched those lips – why, he knew not. He squinted and looked at them so hard that he felt as if he were about to bore a hole in them with his sight.

Then, when the silence of the obelisk room started to creep up at him, he turned and made his way to the stairs.

Most people regarded Jim of Cairo to be wise. Most would argue that his intentions were frequently pure.

But many of his friends knew that, like his talent for poetry, Jim's ability to carry a tune was very small indeed. Perfect musical pitch was something he would never possess.

ᒪᒪᒪᒪᒪ **22** ᒪᒪᒪᒪᒪ

AT THE PANTHEON

HER HOOFS STILL ECHOING clackingly into the still night, Brenda turned another corner. And stōpped.

There in front of her, at the end of the piazza that opened up from her narrow street, stood the majestic Pantheon. Its columns in the front portico gleamed with a greenish-bluish hue as the moonlight shimmered on them.

Brenda lifted her head (her map still in her mouth), and beheld the mighty dome. Perfectly round, its tiles smooth and seamless, it rose up into the dark sky, lit from underneath by rows of faint lights.

Brenda felt her eyelashes tingling, as they nearly always did whenever she was seeing a great building or work of ancient beauty in real life for the first time.

From a few streets away, a clock struck the quarter hour, its chime low and melancholy. Brenda snorted quietly. She knew that she must move now – Time was not to be dallied with.

With her dexterous jaw and tongue, she folded the map into a long strip and slithered it back against her cheek, so that it was fixed under her halter strap, halfway around the back of her neck. Here the map

would be out of the way until she needed it for her return journey to the Palazzo Altemps.

The Wonder Camel made her way across the piazza, being careful not to step in any of the puddles of water where parts of the cobblestones had dipped and sagged. She did not want to enter such an important building with wet hoofs.

Clack-ta-clack-ta-clack-ta-clack. Now that she was walking more slowly, and now that there were no buildings hard-close to her, the noise was not as loud, but the echo still lingered.

She came to the front stairs of the portico. Between the columns, she could see that the doors of the Pantheon were open.

(This did not surprise her, for she had remembered, during her journey here, that the encyclopaedia had mentioned that the Pantheon was always open, and that admission was free all year round.)

She took a calming deep breath, letting the air fill her humps. Then she walked up the stairs and through the doorway.

There was no one around – no guides, no tourists, no living souls at all.

"Rark!" rarked Doris. "Maybe she's gone out to buy herself a new Melodious Tex western adventure novel?"

"Si," said Pasqual, who had woken up when Jim and Doris had come back to the apartment. "I have

SEEN those novels in the bookshops here. They are TRANSLATED into Italian. They are very popular, I understand."

Jim shook his head. "No, I don't think that's where she's gone. To my knowledge, Brenda doesn't read Italian. French, yes, but not Italian…"

"Maybe," said Pasqual, "I should put out a CALL to *la polizia* to search for her. It is a QUIET night – they probably would be GLAD to have a job such as THIS."

"No," Jim said. "Thank you but no. I don't want the sight of a whole lot of police to scare her. Especially all those dark uniforms."

"I understand," Pasqual said, pulling his burgundy-coloured silk dressing-gown around him and shivering.

"It's just not like her to disappear like this," muttered Jim. "Not like her at all…"

Brenda walked slowly into the huge circular interior of the Pantheon, her hoofs clacking with a deep resonance on the marble floor.

The floor itself was something to behold. The marble had been laid in enormous square tiles. Every second tile had a perfect circle inlaid into it, and every other tile was a simple but elegant square within a square.

At four places around the curved walls there stood four tall candelabra. Each of these was filled with a dozen candles, all of them lit. There was just enough light for Brenda to see where she was going.

Slowly she made her way around the walls. Every

now and then she stopped and sniffed the air, trying to sense where Egeria had meant her to look.

All around the walls were groups of columns, no more than three in any one place. Between the columns were beautifully carved niches, many of which had handsome triangular or round-roofed pediments over them.

In these niches, in the flickering candlelight, Brenda saw huge sarcophagi. The colours of these coffins were beautiful, even in the dimness. Green and brown marbles, vivid purple porphyry and sombre orange stonework filled the spaces.

Most of these sarcophagi, Brenda remembered, contain the rulers of Italy. This is where they are resting.

She passed by a large altar set into the wall at the opposite side to the doorway. A row of taller candles was burning here. Brenda smelt the wax and the sweetish smoke and moved quietly on.

The tail, she thought. Where is it?

She continued moving around the Pantheon, bit by bit, past more sarcophagi, one of which contained the remains of the artist Raphael.

All through her journey, silence reigned supreme.

When she came to the doorway again, she turned and made her way to the very centre of the building.

Clack-ta-clack-ta-clack-ta-clack-ta-clack.

She stood in the middle of the circle, in the middle of the exact centre tile of the place, and slowly looked up.

Where is this thing? How do I find it?

Her eyes moved upwards, up into the dome, across the hundreds of big, curved square panels that made up the magnificent hemisphere above. She remembered that the dome was precisely the same height as the width of the Pantheon – 43.3 metres. This is why, she thought, this place is so harmonious … everything is there for everything else.

Her gaze scanned the uppermost reaches of the dome. Here, it was darker than where she was; the candles below had no hope of lighting so high a place. Brenda squinted and peered as far as she was able.

Maybe there is a clue up there, she wondered. On the interior of the dome itself?

There was moonshimmer coming through the oculus, directly above her head. She arched back her neck and looked up through the opening, into the night sky. High above the opening, the moon glowed brightly.

Brenda's neck started to ache, so she took a few steps backwards (still keeping her eyes on the oculus and the moon) so that she would be more comfortable.

All that the lips said, she thought, *was that it was in the Pantheon. There were no more directions, other than that. How am I supposed to—*

Then, in the breath of a nymph, her uncertainty was halted!

Far above, a single beam of moonlight speared down from the sky. It pierced the air in the centre of the oculus and shot to the floor, hitting the spot where Brenda had been standing only a few seconds before.

"Quuuaaaaaaaaooo!"

The Wonder Camel jumped back, amazed at the vibrancy of this single beam. It was no wider than the length of a human's thumb, but it was brighter than all the lights of a football field.

At such close range, the brightness was overwhelming. Brenda snapped her eyelids down over her eyes, to protect them from the blinding glare.

Now, it is a little-known fact that all camels – be they Wonder Camels or ordinary camels, Bactrian or Dromedary – have transparent eyelids. When they are closed, a camel can still see through them.

Luckily, Brenda was a Wonder Camel, and Wonder Camels' eyelids are extra-reflective-protective. They can withstand far greater wind, sandstorms or unexplained freakish moonbeams than an ordinary camel's eyelids. Any ordinary camel would have been partially blinded by this overpowering light.

Brenda stood still, hardly daring to breathe, as the brilliant moonbeam moved back and forth in tiny, hurried patterns on the tile in front of her.

Show me, she thought. *If it is you, show me the way*.

The moonbeam kept moving, as though it was dancing some sort of spindly dance but it couldn't make up its mind which way to go.

Through her closed eyelids, Brenda kept watching it.

The thumb-sized beam stopped briefly, then travelled across the tiled floor until it came to a spot on the curved wall that lay between two of the sarcophagus niches.

Still with her eyes tightly shut, Brenda followed the end of the beam. She watched through her eyelids as it bled slowly up from the floor and onto a place on the wall about half a metre up.

Suddenly the moonlight in the beam increased, getting brighter and brighter, sharper and more intense. There seemed to be a sort of fire now pulsating through the beam. Even through her Wonder Camel eyelids, Brenda could feel the pain entering her eyeballs.

She strained to deflect the brightness, trying to make her eyelids thicker and at the same time trying to keep her focus on the place where the moonbeam was highlighting.

"Quaaooo," she snorted as her eyes felt like they were burning her.

Not giving up, she stared hard at the place on the wall. All she could see was bright, searing whiteness.

Too bright, too blinding!

"Quaaaaaooooo!"

And then it was gone!

The moonbeam disappeared in the inkling of a snort. It did not recede slowly, like a wave rolling back into the ocean. It did not fade and wither until it no longer existed. It simply snapped away into absolutely nothing.

Brenda opened her eyes. For five minutes she could not see, as her sight began to readjust to where she was and what she had just witnessed.

She felt great amounts of sweat on her humps, and heard the quiet all around her. She smelt the age-old aroma of damp marble and cool porphyry and ancient places, but she did not move her recovering eyes from the place where she had last seen the moonbeam.

When she was able to see properly again, she found that she was looking at a part of the Pantheon's wall that she had not seen earlier when she had walked around it. Set into this part of the wall was a small marble tablet, about fifteen centimetres square.

Brenda knelt and lowered herself to the floor, so that her snout was level with this bit of marble on the lower part of the wall. She flapped her eyelashes, getting rid of the last vestiges of the moonbeam and its brightness.

The small marble tablet had a strange inlaid decoration on it: a scattering of tiny, thin lengths of brass. There were dozens of them, set at criss-cross angles all over the place. At first glance, Brenda thought they were miniature arrows, for the end of each bit of brass narrowed to a point, some of which were sharp-looking, others more ornate and a bit rounded.

As Brenda stared at them, she gradually realised they weren't miniature arrows at all. They were hands.

Hands from clocks and watches and other ancient timepieces.

Then she saw the hinges. Two small hinges, maybe as old as the Pantheon itself, were set into the wall along one side of the tablet.

Brenda inspected the opposite side of the tablet. Here, there was a small hole. The Wonder Camel

realised then that it was a keyhole, and that this tablet was actually a small door.

Her heart began thumping excitedly. Quickly she stood, and reversed, and kneeled again. In this position her tail was directly opposite the keyhole.

She snapped her tail into a stiff shaft, and the hairs at the very end of it compressed so that they were as dense and as strong as if they had been made of brass or steel.

Carefully, and as sensitively as she could, she pushed her stiffened tail towards the keyhole. The hairs at the very tip of her tail brushed across the marble door and then touched the rim of the hole.

Brenda took a deep breath and, with intricate precision, she slid the tip of her tail into the hole. It was a tight fit, but in it went.

Now, she thought, with just a bit of wiggling...

She moved her rear flanks about a bit, and the tip of her tail jiggled inside the hole. After a few seconds, there was a loud CLICK.

Brenda snorted with relief and great excitement.

Gently she withdrew her tail from the keyhole. She stood and, with a quick snap, her tail went back to normal. Then she about-turned again so that she was facing the small door, and once more she lowered herself to the floor in front of it.

She moved her snout close to the door. With a soft nuzzle, she pushed at the door, and then moved her snout back.

The small bit of clock-hand-covered marble swung slowly out on its hinges, with an almost inaudible sound, a little like an old, tired wheezing.

Brenda's eyelashes tingled so much she had to take a few deep breaths to try and get them under control. When they were behaving themselves again, she lowered her snout so that she could see into the space on the other side of the door.

Like the door, this space was very small. It was a black, marble-lined box, nothing more.

At the bottom of this box someone had placed a strip of dark crimson silk, older than any silk Brenda had ever seen before.

Lying on this silk was a tiny black sliver, no bigger than a matchstick. Unlike a matchstick, there was an almost microscopic head attached to it.

When Brenda saw the head of the snake, with its jaws opened wide and ready to strike, she knew exactly what she had found.

Her mind raced, and in a matter of seconds she had decided what to do. She stretched back her lips and bared her teeth. Then, holding her breath and being as calm as she knew how, she pushed her teeth into the box in the wall.

Her upper teeth dragged the tail of the Imperishable Bauble of Tiberius out of the box, away from the crimson silk. When the tail was at the very edge of the box, Brenda's tongue whipped into action. Out it came, around the tail it curled.

Into her mouth went the tail.

Brenda arched her tongue, and the tail came to rest underneath it. Then she flattened her tongue on top of it. She had decided that, until she got back to the Palazzo Altemps and to Jim, Doris and Pasqual deLirio, this was the safest and best place for the tail to travel.

The Wonder Camel used her snout to close the door. It locked back into place with a loud CLICK.

Brenda rose and turned to face the doorway of the Pantheon. With a great feeling of exhilaration, she made her way to the exit.

Just before she left the building, she turned and looked up at the oculus. Now she couldn't see the moon through it any more, only the black night sky.

"Quaaaooooo!"

She gave a last snort – a closed-snout snort of thanks and excitement and of salutation – and made her way out into the darkened streets of Rome.

GOTCHA!

"WHAT I DON'T understand," croaked Desdemona, riding Bone's fez as he strode along the gloomy street, "is why you just didn't go and grab the Bauble off her! Why waste time, promisin' to get Cairo Jim and his stupid friends?"

"Because, you slow swag of sardonic stupidity, I am *intrigued*."

"In *what*?"

"She mentioned that Jim stole something from her. With my natural traits of Genius, I am incredibly curious to find out what he took. Only by delivering him to her will my curiosity be assuaged."

"I reckon we shoulda just took it. I coulda pecked her all over until she gave in and dropped it. What a wasted opportunity! Sheesh!"

"No," said Bone. "Besides, by delivering Jim to her I will have an added satisfaction – the satisfaction of him seeing me, his hated adversary, obtain possession of the Bauble. That'll turn his pith helmet green, I have no doubt."

"Can I ask you a question?"

"Oh, but of course, Desdemona. There is nothing I would rather do right now than answer your

pertinent and incisive queries." He puffed a column of cigar smoke upwards at her, and turned a corner into a small, dingy alleyway.

When she had finished coughing, she asked, "How in the heck are we gonna find Jim? This city's big, y'know. What're you planning on doin' – standin' on a street corner and waitin' for him to walk past?"

"No, you gormless git. I plan to start immediately. I would say, using my fine detective skills and my knowledge of the character of Cairo Jim, that he has been put up in some ritzy hotel by Gerald Perry Esquire. That man's got more money than he knows what to do with. The imbecile."

"A hotel, eh?"

"Arrrr."

"Which one?"

"That I know not. At least not at this stage. But all the good hotels are open all night. There is always someone on the front desk, right around the clock."

"So?"

"So we shall enter every four- and five-star hotel we pass and, by pretending that I am Cairo Jim's near and dear brother, Aubrey, I shall find out from the person on the front desk if Jim is staying at that particular hotel."

"Aubrey? I never knew he had a brother called Aubrey. Jeez, what was his mother thinkin' when she called him that?"

"He doesn't have a brother called Aubrey, slughead. I am using the moniker just as an example."

"*Monica?* He has a brother called Monica? That's a seriously weird family, a very weird—"

"If you don't shut up, I shall have you taxidermied first thing in the morning."

"Crark."

For a minute she said nothing, as Bone walked down the alleyway, searching for a shortcut to the expensive hotels near the Piazza Navona. Then she croaked, "I have another question. What exactly are you gonna do when you've got this Bobble?"

"Oh, I have a plan, Desdemona," he answered, his voice rumbling with deep ambition. "A plan of greater Genius perhaps than any of my other plans to date."

"What? Whatisit?"

He stopped walking and reached deep into the pocket of his plus-fours. From out of it he took a neatly folded newspaper.

"What?" Desdemona rasped, eyeballing it. "Ya gonna do the crossed words or somethin'?"

"No, you execrable end-product of evolution. This is the newspaper that Cairo Jim left in my cell when he visited me in that dire prison. His carelessness will cost him – and the entire world – their future freedom!"

"Whaddya mean?"

"I mean that here" – he began unfolding the paper to show her – "I read about a meeting that is soon to take place in Rome. A very important meeting. And if things go according to my plan, it will be a meeting that will secure me my place as leader of the entire planet."

The raven's eyes throbbed hard.

"If everything falls into place – and I have an instinct deep down inside that fortune is favouring me right now – then within a few short days every nation in the world will be bowing to me. Every leader of every country will be worshipping me. Every—"

There he stopped, clutching the paper tightly and looking up into the night.

"What's the matter?" Desdemona said. "Has the sphinx got your tongue?"

"Listen!" he hissed. *"Fortune is indeed smiling upon me!"*

Desdemona cocked her head and listened. "What? I don't hear—"

"SHHH!"

She kept silent.

For several seconds she heard nothing except for a tap dripping away somewhere near the end of the alley.

Then, travelling on the muted air of the night, came a faint echo.

Clack-ta-clack-ta-clack-ta-clack…

"What is it?" she asked Bone.

"Hoofsteps." He folded the newspaper again and shoved it into his pocket.

"Hoofsteps?"

"Echoing through the streets. Thank Hesperus for this resonating city!"

"So what?"

"Listen, glue-ears. Hear the *sort* of hoofsteps they are."

Clack-ta-clack-ta-clack-ta-clack ... the sound was not as far away now.

"I give in," she sighed. "What sort are they?"

"They are the footsteps of a camel," Bone whispered, his eyes filling with glee. "And not any ordinary camel. That's a Wonder Camel walking out there!"

"Ya mean...?"

"Arrrr. It seems we won't have to interrogate any hotel staff after all. Oh, what a night this is turning out to be!"

Clack-ta-clack-ta-clack-ta-clack...

"It's gettin' closer."

"Help me listen, Desdemona. Help me to determine if she's alone."

In silence, man and raven listened.

"She's by herself, all right," said Desdemona. "I can't hear any other footsteps."

"Nor can I. Can you detect any wing beats?"

Once more, Desdemona listened. "Nope. There's no smartyfeathers macaw flyin' along with her."

"And we can't hear any echoes of talking, can we? Knowing what a chatterbeak that Dolly-bird is, if she were with the camel, she'd be screeching her head off."

Clack-ta-clack-ta-clack-ta-clack...

"Where do ya reckon she is?" Desdemona's eyes throbbed malevolently.

"Hard to tell. These echoes are usually very deceptive. But we must be ready, Desdemona. We must be prepared to capture her with the minimum of fuss.

Then Cairo Jim will have no choice but to meet us – and that Bottnoff woman – tomorrow evening."

"Crark."

Bone scoured the end of the alleyway. "Bingo!" he whispered.

"What? Have ya seen her?"

"Not yet, but I've seen something which will help us restrain the Wonder Camel. She's a big beast, and liable to kick out at us when we try and capture her. But if we cover her head, she will become confused. I know for a fact that a confused Wonder Camel remains calm until it has thought through its predicament. By that time we will have restrained her fully, and she won't be able to fight us."

"How're we gonna cover her head? You gonna take off your trousers and throw 'em at her?"

"Heaven forbid!"

"Phew!"

"No, see down there, above that shop doorway? There is a canvas awning. Come, let us hurry."

Clack-ta-clack-ta-clack-ta-clack…

Bone ran to the end of the alleyway, with Desdemona perched on his fez. He stopped at the large, green-and-white-striped canvas awning.

"Right, Desdemona, get up there. Use that razor-sharp beak of yours to slice the canvas from its frame. I'll catch it when it falls. Then cut away those awning ropes and bring them to me."

"Aye, aye, my Captain."

She flew off his fez and onto the awning.

Bone watched her as she hacked and sawed her way through the canvas, all the while keeping his ears open for the echoes of Brenda's hoofsteps.

Clack-ta-clack-ta-clack-ta-clack...

In three minutes, the bulk of the canvas had been cut away from the frame. Bone caught it as it fell, and quickly bundled it up under his arm.

"For once, you've done well. Now the ropes. And hurry! I believe she's just around the corner or two!"

Desdemona swooped at the four ropes and sliced them clean away from the frame, delivering each to Bone as she did so.

He slung the ropes over his shoulder. "Now," he whispered, "here's what you must do..."

Clack-ta-clack-ta-clack-ta-clack...

Two streets away from the vandalised shop front, Brenda was in a lather. She had consulted the map just after she had left the Pantheon but, in her excitement at what had happened to her, she didn't check where her northern point was. She had no idea that she had been holding the map the wrong way up.

Now she was hopelessly lost. Instead of making her way directly back to the Palazzo Altemps, she had wandered closer to the ruins of the Forum Romana.

She felt the tiny head of the Imperishable Bauble underneath her tongue. At least she knew where *that* was.

She came to the end of another narrow street,

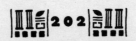

and decided to turn left. Whichever way she had turned, it would have been the wrong way.

"SCCCCRAAAAAAAAAAAAARRRKKKKKKK!"

Suddenly a flurry of foul, greasy, stinking feathers and sharp, lethal claws shot about her head!

"QUAAAAAAAAAAAAAOOOOOOOO!"

Brenda rose up onto her rear hoofs, keeping her mouth firmly shut to protect what was inside it.

"ARRRRRRRRRR!"

Darkness plunged down onto her head – heavy, stiff darkness, and her hoofs returned to the ground.

"The ropes, Desdemona, the ropes!"

The darkness got tighter around her head and neck, as the raven flew around Brenda and lashed one of the ropes about the canvas.

"Quaaaaaaaauuuuuuggghhhh!"

Now Brenda felt her rear flanks being coiled and tied so that she was unable to take large steps, let alone run.

"She's trussed enough, Captain," came a hoarse cry.

"Arrrr. Hurry, let's go before we're seen."

Bone grabbed the rope that was around the canvas covering Brenda's head and snout. Brenda felt a sharp yank and, having no choice, she moved jerkily forwards.

"Where we goin' to?" Desdemona flapped her wings and came to perch on Brenda's fore hump. "Where can we take her – she's so BIG!"

"To the Colosseum," Bone answered. "I cannot think of a more fitting place for the final hours of Jim of Cairo. Arrrrrrr!"

A DIFFERENT
SORT OF DARKNESS

WHEN THE CANVAS WAS UNBOUND from Brenda's head, she found herself in a big, half-decayed chamber with one of its walls exposed to the night outside.

She was sitting on the cold, dank, earth floor of this chamber. Her rear legs were still trussed beneath her, and now her front legs were similarly tied. A rough rope had been fastened around her neck, and the other end was connected to an ancient bronze ring halfway up the opposite wall.

"Quaaaaooooooo!" she snorted angrily.

"There's no use making a fuss," sneered Neptune Bone, a Belch of Brouhaha hanging from his wide lips. "In here, no one can hear you snort!"

Brenda squared her jaw and directed a fierce look at him. She tried to squirm upwards, but there was no way she could stand – her folded and tied legs were holding her like bulldog clips.

Then, by the light of a small candle burning in a niche in one of the walls, she saw something ... something in Bone's pudgy hands.

"Any clues?" rasped Desdemona, perched on a low part of the wall next to him.

Bone studied the map he had pulled from Brenda's bridle after he had uncovered her head. "Arrr," he murmured. "Let us see…"

Brenda watched him as his eyes slid across the map like two drunken tadpoles on an ice-rink.

All at once, the two drunken tadpoles lit up. "I am indeed blessed," Bone said, puffing away at the cigar. "Look, bird, here on the map. Someone has put a circle around a spot on the Piazza Sant'Apollinaire."

"What's it mean?" Desdemona croaked.

"That I am not sure of right – wait just a momento! Look, here in the margin! See? That's the handwriting, the neat, carefully made, goody-goody-oh-I-never-smudge-*my*-writing, of Jim of Cairo!"

"Mr Poetry?"

"The very wretch!"

Brenda felt her eyelashes filling with dread.

"Whatsit say?" scrarked the raven. "Whatsit say?"

Bone held the map at arm's length, and read aloud the address that was written there: "'Palazzo Altemps Museum, Piazza Sant'Apollinaire, northern end of the Piazza Navona.' Then there's a name or something: 'Professor deLirio.'"

"Quaaooo!"

"Professor deLirio?" repeated Desdemona, her red eyes throbbing with confusion. "Who's he?"

Bone's memory jerked, and the image of the neatly dressed Pasqual deLirio, with his natty bow-tie and elegant trousers, rushed into his head. "He used to

lecture us at Archaeology School. He was a fastidious, sensitive, squealing sort of man, very keen on ancient Italian history."

He took a deep drag on the cigar and let the smoke issue languidly from his mouth. "I remember now – when he retired, he came to live in Rome. At some museum or other. I'll bet my last fez that it's the Palazzo Altemps. And I bet that that's where we'll find Cairo Jim and that macaw."

"Smartyfeathers!"

"Arrrrrr." Bone smiled a smile of such superciliousness that Brenda almost felt her humps turn. "How fortunate that I still have Ms Bottnoff's mobile phone with me. Now listen, Desdemona, you must do something at once!"

"Oh, not that little dance you make me perform, with them grapes and those cuttlefish behind my—"

"Don't be absurd! No, fly out and find one of those public phone booths, one that has a telephone book in it. Grab the book and high-tail it back here!"

"But that'll be heavy," she objected. She pecked at a flea biting her under the wing. "I'll get a hernia if I try and fly back here with—"

"I don't care what else you get, only get the phone book first!"

His arm shot out and he grabbed the raven by her throatfeathers. Swiftly he lobbed her out into the night, where she tumbled beak over talons in the air before righting herself and flying off.

"And don't come back empty-clawed," Bone yelled after her.

Brenda wriggled her rear flanks, swishing her tail against the cold, hard floor.

"Be still, you dumb beast," Bone snarled at her. He blew smoke into her eyes, and sat back against the wall. "And wait for the final showdown, when the world that you have known and lived in will become nothing but a pathetic, pale memory of primeval paradise!"

An hour later, the phone in Pasqual's apartment rang, shrilly, like a small creature screaming.

Pasqual rushed to answer it.

Jim bolted from the chaise longue, Doris clinging to his shoulder as if she were part of him.

"Pronto," said Pasqual into the receiver. "Mi scusi, posso…"

Pasqual cupped the receiver in his hand and held it away from his face. "It's a man," he told Jim and Doris. "He's asking for you, Cairo Jim."

Jim's palms began to grow moist. He took the phone from Pasqual. Doris fluttered onto Pasqual's shoulder, and both of them watched Jim as he listened to the voice on the other end.

"You've WHAT?" cried the archaeologist-poet. "You filthy, thieving … all right, yes, I'll listen."

Doris saw Jim's forehead becoming beaded with perspiration.

At last, after what seemed like an eternity and a day,

Jim said, "We'll be ready. But I just want to say one thing. If anything happens to her, I swear, I'll hunt you down. I'll travel to the ends of this earth to find you. And when I do, you WILL know the taste of justice!"

Doris and Pasqual heard a loud noise on the other end. It sounded like a man blowing a very fierce raspberry into the phone.

Jim listened for a second or two more, then put down the receiver.

"Brenda?" was all that Doris could say.

"She's been camelnapped. By Bone."

"Scraaaaaaark! Bone?"

"Neptune Bone?" said Pasqual.

"He escaped from prison. He's going to call us late tonight, to tell us where to meet if we ever want to see her again."

"Where *is* she?" Doris screeched.

"I don't know. He said he'd tell us the meeting-place when he called later."

Jim sat on the chaise longue and cradled his forehead. The archaeologist-poet felt as if he had had all the energy, all the life force, all the enthusiasm that surged about inside him drained out completely.

Doris hop-fluttered off Pasqual's shoulder and went to be by Jim's side. She said nothing, but pressed herself close to his leg. Her mind was flurrying with worry.

"Let us hope," Pasqual said, his voice a tremor of dreadful uncertainty, "that he also does not have the Bauble. Or, heaven help us, its tail."

Jim shuddered. Some things were far too terrible to contemplate.

The morning passed slowly for Brenda. The only good thing was that the ground beneath her had warmed a little. By noon, she no longer felt the dampness of the earth.

Bone and Desdemona had left her for a while, mid-morning, to go out and find something to eat. She had remained in the gloomy chamber, her head and shoulders covered with the shop-awning canvas, her legs still tied under her.

She knew that she was in a chamber – one of the many half-ruined chambers – of the Colosseum. She knew because when she had been captured, Bone had said that that was where he was taking her. This had been reconfirmed when she had heard a tourist walking by her chamber, reading out loud from a guide book:

"Says in here that this Colosseum 'was the scene for huge shows of gladiator combat and extravaganzas that had exotic animals from all around the world. Lions, tigers, elephants, Emnobellian Jungle Donkeys, apes and many more. When the Colosseum was opened, the games lasted for 100 days and nights, and 5000 animals were killed. At one gladiator show staged by the emperor Trajan, more than 9000 fighters were slaughtered...'"

Brenda was shuddering by the time the tourist's voice had died away.

Early in the afternoon, her canvas was removed. She blinked and saw the large, round outline of Bone and the scraggly feathers of Desdemona in front of her.

"Arrr. Slowly the day wears on." Bone lowered himself into the corner and made himself as comfortable as he could against the ancient wall. He had a thick blanket with him, and a plump rose-red cushion. Brenda deduced that he must have stolen them from some shop, as they still had their price-tags attached.

"Keep an eye on the beast," Bone said to Desdemona. He settled himself onto the blanket, taking off his fez and resting his greasy head on the cushion. "I'm going to get a few hours of shut-eye. And if any tourists show their faces – not that I think they will, for I purposely chose the dingiest and most remote chamber in the Colosseum – give them the fright of their sorry little lives."

Desdemona belched (she had feasted on three stolen tins of imported Japanese seaweed) and watched him as he fell asleep.

When he was snoring steadily, the raven hopped down off the low part of the wall and paraded herself in front of Brenda.

"So," she croaked. "Who's the clever Wonder Camel now, eh?"

Brenda watched the black bird strut across the floor.

"Wonder Camel, my tarsus! You know what you are?"

Brenda snorted nothing.

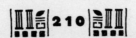

"I'll tell you what you are. You're a *Dunder* Camel! Dunder, dunder, dunder!" She poked out her rough yellow tongue and waggled it at Brenda.

Still, Brenda made no snort. She willed herself to sit there as calmly as she could.

"You're not so clever," taunted Desdemona, hopping close to Brenda. "You're not so smart. If you were clever and smart, ya wouldn't be here in this Colossaleum, would ya, with yer legs tied up?"

Brenda kept watching the bird, keeping her eyes on the sharp beak that was inching closer.

"Dunderhead, dummy, Brenda the bozo! Crark!"

Brenda made herself remember a rhyme she had learned when she was a calf: *"Sticks and stones may bruise my humps, but names will never make me jump."*

"You and your little buddies. You get in our way every single time. You and your stupid quest for goodness. Well, I got news for you, baby: this is the modern world. There ain't no such thing as *goodness.* That went out with typewriters!"

Brenda's mane started to hackle. She had always had a fondness for typewriters. She pressed her tongue down hard and kept her mouth shut.

"Dumb-dumb," rasped Desdemona. "Idiot-snout!"

Then Desdemona narrowed her eyes, which seemed to make them throb more fiercely. "Hey! Ya listenin' to me? Ya moron, ya can't ignore me an' get away with it! I'll show you what I'm made of!" And she lunged forward and jabbed at Brenda with the tip of her beak.

Brenda felt a sudden prick of searing pain. She shut her eyes tightly.

"C'mon, ya dumb animal! Snort!"

Another sudden jab of beak caught Brenda in the front of her chest. She gasped, and opened her eyes.

Desdemona danced about, her eyes wide and cruel. "Snort! Snort, snort, snort!"

In came the beak again, punching Brenda just below her neck. This time the air was knocked out of her throat.

Without thinking, Brenda lifted her head, opened her mouth, and snorted – a fierce, loud snort of fear and warning.

"*Quuuuuuaaaaaaaaaaaaaaaaaaaaaaaaoooo!*"

And there was a sound on the hard, earth floor.

Dlink!

"Heh, heh," sniggered Desdemona. "Knew I could make ya—" her eyes caught on the thing that had fallen out of Brenda's mouth and which now lay in front of her. "Hello, what have we here?"

She crouched down and used her beak to turn over the tiny, dark object.

"Looks like a snake … a little snake. Frozen stiff."

"QUUUUUUAAAAAAAAAAAAAAAAAOOOO!"

Brenda's snort was louder this time; louder but desperate.

Loud enough to wake Bone.

"What in the name of Ethel Merman—?" He rolled over and sat up. "Desdemona! Are you tormenting that idiotic camel?"

"Look, my Captain. Look what came outta her mouth!"

"I have no interest in the saliva of a camel," he mumbled, scowling distastefully. "If I want to look at brainless matter, I only have to look at—"

"No, no, no!" Desdemona pecked up the tail of the Imperishable Bauble and hopped over to Bone. She spat it onto his plus-fours. "Look! Whatisit?"

Brenda watched helplessly.

Bone lowered his tangly eyebrows. He picked up the tiny tail and turned it over and over between his thumb and forefinger. The opened mouth of the miniature snake, stretched wide and furious, impressed him with its savageness.

"If this is what I think it is," he purred, like a great, overfed cat who has just discovered an upturned cream truck, "then tonight, at thirty minutes after midnight, my dreams will take on a hugeness that not even *I* have dared think of. Oh, the sweetness of my fortune is almost too, too great for me to bear!"

Desdemona listened, curious.

"Tonight," Bone said, his breath hardly heavier than the air in the chamber, "I shall finally strut along the avenue of everlasting greatness. Arrrrrrr!"

And Brenda felt her humps go hollow with hopelessness.

⑤⑤⑤⑤⑤ **25** ⑤⑤⑤⑤⑤

AT THE COLOSSEUM

AT TEN MINUTES TO MIDNIGHT, the silence in Pasqual's apartment was shattered by the urgent, shrill ringing of his telephone.

"YOU get it, Jim," Pasqual said. "It will be for you."

Cairo Jim's fingers were trembling as he picked up the receiver.

Doris's feathers were bristling with indignation and anger.

"Hello?" Jim said. He listened for a few seconds, then put the receiver down.

"Well?" flapped Doris. "What do we do? How's Bren?"

"If we want to see her again," answered the archaeologist-poet, "we have to be at the Colosseum in forty minutes. There'll be a candle burning to show us where we have to go."

Pasqual checked his elegant wristwatch. "Forty MINUTES? Then we must HURRY! I'll get my COAT!"

Jim put on his pith helmet (the smell of roses filled the apartment) and smoothed down the front of his shirt. "Come on, my dear," he said to Doris. "We're not beaten yet."

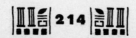

The macaw flew to his shoulder, but her beak was without words.

Meltem Bottnoff, formerly of the Antiquities Squad of Turkey, paced up and down by the Temple of Saturn in the Forum Romana.

It was now 12.20 a.m. She had arrived early, not being able to contain her eagerness at the thought of seeing Cairo Jim again. Her corduroy slacks swished urgently in the damp air.

Presently there was a hushed *whoop-whoop-whoop*. She looked up to see the dark, fluttering form of Desdemona hovering above her. Only the raven's eyes stood out against the blackened sky.

"Where is Jim?" called Meltem. "And where is your master? He promised me—"

"Hang onto your horseradish. I got a message for ya."

"Well?"

"Captain Bone says you hafta be at the Colosalleum in ten minutes. It's just down the road."

"I know where the Colosseum is. Where will I find him in there?" she asked. "It is enormous."

"There's a candle burnin'. Go to that. And don't forget to bring the Bobble."

Desdemona made a sound, part snigger and part belch. Then she took off at great speed towards the Colosseum.

Meltem did up her coat and made her way there as well.

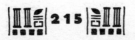

★ ★ ★

The outside of the Colosseum, lit by rows of muted electric lamps, appeared before Jim, Doris and Pasqual deLirio as they turned the final corner.

"Rark. There 'tis."

"And in there," Jim whispered, "is where we find Brenda."

"I HOPE she is all RIGHT," said Pasqual in a muted voice (for him at least).

"Jim?"

"What, my dear?"

"I've got an idea."

Jim and Pasqual kept walking, while Doris rode on Jim's shoulder.

"Tell us," said Jim.

"I'm going to fly off, separately to you and Pasqual. I don't know why, but something tells me there'll be more strength for us if we're not all together when we march in there."

Jim frowned. "Do you think that's wise?"

Doris clucked her beak as she considered it. "I've just got this feeling," she answered at last. "Don't worry, I'll still be in there with you, only not *close* to you. I'm going to keep a bird's-eye view on everything."

"Be careful, my dear," said the archaeologist-poet.

"And if I spy something before you and Pasqual, I'll come and let you know. Any danger, for example. That Bone is devious. There's no telling what he's got up the sleeve of that badly designed shirt of his!"

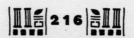

Jim reached up and rubbed her yellow chestfeathers gently. He could feel her little heart beating hard against her ribs. "For your foresight, I am always more grateful than I can ever say," he said soothingly.

"Well, we're a team, aren't we?" she prowked.

"There," said Pasqual, nodding ahead. "There is the ENTRANCE to the Colosseum. Don't worry, you two, BRENDA will be there for us."

In the centre of the vast and overgrown open-air auditorium of the once-mighty Colosseum, Neptune Flannelbottom Bone waited smugly and impatiently.

In his fingers, he grasped the tail. To him, right now, it was the most precious object in all the world.

He was alone down there, in the middle of the enormity – alone with his thoughts and ambitions. These were bristling through his hide with such force it was as though a constant surge of lightning was continually travelling throughout his body.

Soon, he thought to himself, everything would be as it had always been meant to be. In a few very short minutes, he would at last have enough power at his fingertips – enough invincible, unyielding power to convey him into the realm of Ruler of the World. All he needed was that Bauble. And then, in one day's time, he would disrupt the meeting that was to be held—

"SCRAAAAAAAAAARK!" came a cry from one of the chambers far above him. He looked up into the gloom.

"What is it, you atrocious, alarming annoyance?"

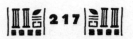

"It's the dame," squawked Desdemona. "She's comin' now, through the entrance arch to yer right!"

"Arrrr. Be quiet up there, until I need you."

"Aye, aye, my Captain."

Bone bent over and lit a wide, knee-high candle which he had positioned next to him on a broken marble tile. He straightened and turned.

"WHERE IS JIM OF CAIRO?" came a sudden voice, echoing around the ruins.

Bone nearly stepped back into the candle. "Madam," he said, "do not worry. He will be here any moment."

"You promised me," Meltem Bottnoff said, her eyes wide and saucer-like, her cheeks pale and almost alabaster-translucent against her dark hair.

"Do not worry," Bone said. "Have you brought the Bauble?"

"When I see Cairo Jim, then you shall see the Bauble, Captain Bone."

"When I hand you Cairo Jim, you will hand me the Bauble, madam."

"As we agreed," she said. Slowly she turned and looked all around the immense tiers of seats and chambers and viewing galleries, all of them crumbled by Time and smothered by the thick darkness. "This is a place of such sadness," she said quietly. "So much was lost or destroyed here…"

"But, madam," Bone sneered, "think of *tonight*! Such wealth and dreams will be gained here!"

She brought her faraway gaze back to his face, and her

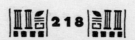

eyes narrowed. "We shall see," she said. "We shall see."

At that moment, Bone heard something. "Sh! Footsteps!"

Meltem froze, and Bone raised his head, as if that would help him hear better. He moved around until he was standing between Meltem and the direction where he believed the footsteps were coming from. His ample shadow completely obscured her from being illuminated by the candlelight.

Into the auditorium, emerging quickly from the darkness at the edges, came Cairo Jim, followed by Pasqual deLirio.

"Arrrr. Send in the clowns."

Jim saw the candle almost straight away. With long steps he bounded across the rough ground to confront Bone.

"You hubristic brute!" he shouted, his face red with the anger that was consuming him. "Where's Brenda?"

Bone sneered at him. "Hello, Jim. There's someone I think you should meet."

He stepped aside. There in front of Jim stood Meltem Bottnoff, trembling and pale.

She looked up at the archaeologist-poet, and smelled the odour from his pith helmet. "The sweet smell of roses," she whispered. "Still it comes…"

"M-Ms Bottnoff," Jim stammered. "We haven't seen—"

"BONE!" cried Pasqual deLirio. "Where is Brenda the WONDER Camel?"

Bone's eyes flashed at Meltem. "Madam, I have kept my end of the bargain. There is Cairo Jim. Now, I believe you have a little something for me?"

Without taking her gaze from the face of Jim, Meltem reached into the pocket of her blazer and withdrew her closed fist.

Bone held out his fat hand. "Give, give, give," he panted.

Meltem opened her fist above his palm. There was a small *dlink* as the Imperishable Bauble of Tiberius fell into it.

"Arrrrrr," he moaned, almost in ecstasy. Then he raised his head and called out: "DROP AND BIND, Desdemona!"

The events of the next five seconds were a blur in the darkness: down swooped the raven with an enormous, thick rope trailing from her beak, Bone shoved Meltem and Jim back-to-back and held Pasqual against them so that his back was wedged against their sides, then Bone stepped quickly back away from them. Desdemona flew around the trio at incredible speed, lashing the rope tightly around their shoulders, then their waists – at the same time securing their arms to their sides – then their legs. Finally their ankles were bound.

Bone crouched down and tied the toughest sailors' knots he knew. When he had done this, he stood and stepped back, gloating and superior.

"You villainous dreg of humanity," Jim yelled.

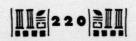

"Where's Brenda?"

"Let there be light," Bone said. "Look, you pathetic posse, up there. On that ledge near the top of the amphitheatre!"

Jim, Meltem and Pasqual craned their necks and looked up. Far above, a small candle came to life.

There was not much light coming from that candle, but Jim could just make out the shape of Desdemona hopping away from it. Next to it he also saw the bound, trussed figure of Brenda.

"Brenda!" he cried, as loudly as he could.

"Quaaaoooo!" came her desperate reply.

"Look above her," Bone said tauntingly. "You see that large piece of rock suspended from that rope? Directly above her head? It used to be part of one of the thousands of steps in this place, you know."

"You monstrous—" began Jim.

"Don't even *think* of trying to escape," Bone snapped. "If the three of you so much as move from the spot upon which you are all standing, if you budge one single centimetre, the raven up there severs that rope. The rock crashes down. And the camel is brained beyond usefulness!"

Meltem could sense Jim's shoulders sag behind her, as could Pasqual.

"And now," Bone said, "there is a matter to be brought before the court."

"The COURT?" repeated Pasqual, and Bone jumped slightly at his urgent voice.

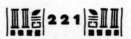

"Arrrr. Tonight, I am the judge. And I preside over a case of theft, Cairo Jim."

"What do you mean?" asked Jim, his throat getting tighter by the second.

"Tell him, madam."

Meltem was silent.

"Tell him what you told me yesterday. That Jim of Cairo stole something from you and now you want it back."

"I never!" shouted Jim. "You lie, Bone! I've never stolen anything in my life!"

Bone came close to them, and snarled menacingly into Meltem's face. "Did you or did you not inform me that Cairo Jim stole something from you?"

Meltem swallowed. Then she spoke in a quiet, sad voice. "I did. But it's not what you are thinking, Captain Bone. It wasn't anything you can *touch* that he took from me. Not anything you can pick up and hold in your hand…"

"Like the Imperishable Bauble of Tiberius, perhaps?" Bone held the Bauble before her eyes, and the eyes of Jim and Pasqual.

"No!" groaned Jim, his shoulders sagging further.

"No," Meltem said. "It was not Jim's fault he took what he did."

"What did I take?" Jim asked, totally flummoxed.

Meltem moved her hand back, only a centimetre or two, for that was all she could move it. Gently it touched the back of Jim's hand. "It was my heart," she whispered.

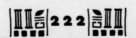

Bone's eyebrows shot upwards.

"Well swoggle me with serenades," gasped Jim. "You mean—"

"Couldn't you tell, Jim?" asked Meltem. "All the time we shared in Turkey, couldn't you tell?"

Jim's forehead and the back of his neck were running with moisture. "I-I-I'm sorry, Meltem, I had no idea."

"It is not your fault." She felt the heat in his hand. "When we said goodbye, something changed in me. Something was missing. It was as though something had been plucked from deep within me. I became … a different person. I knew I had to see you again, to spend more time with you."

"And so she stole this," Bone gloated. "To entice you to come to Rome and see her. Oh, how bilge-making!"

"Shut that garbage-strewing mouth of yours!" shouted Jim.

Like a great, obese panther, Bone sprang around so that he was face to face with his enemy. "You have offended me for the last time, Jim of Cairo. You will never live to see my most brilliant success. For tonight you shall die."

"What do you mean, your 'most brilliant success'? What are you talking about, you deranged lunatic?"

Bone tucked the Bauble into his waistcoat pocket and took out, from his trousers pocket, the folded newspaper. This he opened in front of them, slowly and deliberately.

"I mean," he purred, "listen to this…"

THE PLAN FOR THE WORLD TO COME...

THE ROPES THAT BOUND Jim, Meltem and Pasqual seemed to be growing tighter, as they listened to Bone read a headline from the paper.

"'GLOBAL TOTAL AND BINDING PEACE TREATY OF PERPETUITY TO BE SIGNED IN ROME ON 21 APRIL'. How do you like them apples?"

"What are you talking about?" Jim said.

Bone threw the newspaper onto the ground. "April the twenty-first is tomorrow, Mr Goody-Gumbum. And tomorrow, every single President from every single country, every single Prime Minister, Queen, King, Emir, Grand Chief, Emperor, Empress, Governor, Party Leader, General and every other Person-in-Charge from around the world will be gathering in Rome to sign this Global Total and Binding Peace Treaty of Perpetuity."

Far above, Brenda strained to hear what was going on.

"This Treaty," Bone continued, "is supposed to put an end to wars for ever. It is designed to quell unrest and conflicts. It is supposed to set up the world to be all goodness and wonderfulness and sweety-sweety-cuteness. How ridiculous!"

"SO?" blurted Pasqual deLirio. "What is this to do with YOU?"

"Everything, Professor Squealer. You see, now that I have the Bauble, I shall change their plans."

Jim's blood ran cold, as if ice had all at once entered his veins and stalled his heartbeat. "What are you going to do?"

"Arrrr, as soon as the last of these important personages has put their signature to this worthless document, I shall steal a few seconds. A few seconds is all I need to change the beginning of the document so that it shall no longer be a Treaty, but a Contract."

"Oh!" Meltem gasped.

"A signed Contract that will grant me, Neptune Flannelbottom Bone, power over the entire world. That shall give me exclusive rights to all the world's resources – gold, diamonds, macadamia nuts, as many free manicures as I want. That will enable me to wipe out whole countries at my whim, to destroy all those sinister rainforests, to imprison and dispose of anyone who gets in my way, to introduce new taxes on books and learning! To abolish charities! And this Contract will have been signed by every important person present tomorrow!"

As Jim listened to Bone's megalomaniacal rantings, the ice in his veins turned to molten lead. He was boiling with fury. "You're deluded!" he shouted. "Think about it, Bone, you'll never get away with it. They'll see what you've done straight away, and throw you in the deepest pit there is!"

"Oh they will, will they?"

"Of course they will. It's you against all those people. One man against all of them! They won't have come alone, you know. No, they'll have their bodyguards and their soldiers and their ladies-in-waiting. You'll be apprehended faster than you can sneer!"

Bone thrust his face so close to Cairo Jim's that his bulbous nose pressed against the archaeologist-poet's. "DO YOU THINK I HAVEN'T THOUGHT OF THAT?" he screamed, his prune-smelling breath rushing over Jim and Meltem and Pasqual.

Jim said nothing.

Bone stepped back. "Of course they'd have me arrested, quick-smart. If I were only able to stop Time for a matter of *seconds*, and if it were just me *on my own*, my power would be fragile. Not worth a pinch. But look, you wretches. Look what I will be able to do with what I've got..."

He took out the Bauble in his right hand, and held it above his head. Then, with his left hand, he reached into his waistcoat pocket and withdrew the tail.

He raised the tail in his left hand. "With the Bauble intact, reunited with its tail, it won't just be *me* against the world..."

"The tail?" Jim whispered.

Pasqual nodded. "SI."

"He has the tail!" cried Meltem, horrified.

"I shall be able to not only *stop* Time, but also to turn it back. I will never grow old! I will rule for as long as

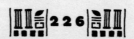

I want, which shall be for ever. Now you know why they call this the Eternal City! Arrr!"

Bone brought his hands together with deliberation that was almost unbearable to watch. When the tail made contact with the Bauble, a small beam of bright green light shot out from the lion's hind regions.

There was a loud GLICK, and the tail snapped into place on the back of the Imperishable Bauble of Tiberius.

"I have your camel to thank for that," Bone told them.

"Quaaaoooooo!" snorted Brenda, high above.

"Shut it," rasped Desdemona, hopping about next to her. "Or that rock'll come crashin' down, and then it's Goodnight, Irene!"

"No, Cairo Jim, it won't just be *me* present tomorrow. After I have changed the Treaty to my Governing Contract, I shall have the support of the Past..."

"OF ALL THE CALAMITIES OF LOST HISTORY!" exclaimed Pasqual deLirio, trembling uncontrollably.

"Arrrr," said Bone, his heart racing at Pasqual's ferocious despair. "That's one way of looking at it, Professor. But there is a *better* way for you to truly comprehend what power I shall have at my fingertips. Let me *show* you what force will accompany me tomorrow."

"No!" cried Jim. "Not here! Not with all the souls that perished in this place!"

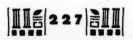

Bone hurried to the far side of the auditorium. "Don't any of you move a muscle," he threatened, "or the camel is burger meat!"

Swiftly (for a man so large) he vaulted the first tier of stone seats. Then he held the Bauble and the tail to his lips, and uttered into it – a mixture of Latin and other words he knew; an invocation to the buried secrets of the past.

"Now the show's underway," Desdemona muttered, forgetting all about her chomping fleas.

Brenda squirmed … her heart was almost beating through her ribcage.

Everything in the centre of the auditorium was suddenly still. No wind blew, no cat miaowed. The silence was as heavy as the stonework.

"Jim?" said Meltem.

"Yes, Meltem?"

"I'm sorry."

Jim rubbed his hand against hers. "There's nothing to be sorry about," he said. "Our hearts are things that are bigger than we are."

"OH, BY THE IDES OF MARCH!" screamed Pasqual. "LOOK! LOOK! OVER THERE!"

At the far end of the auditorium, a strange glow was coming out of the ground. Long, spindly beams of intense, bluish light pushed upwards, splaying in all directions as if they were trying to burst forth from the darkness underneath.

"It is happening!" Bone screamed, his beard bristling

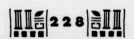

with raw amazement. "THE POWER IS MINE AT LAST!"

The light was growing stronger, bluer, brighter, and now something else was happening: from far away, under the earth it seemed, came the sound of gravelly trumpet blasts.

"Trumpets?" cried Jim.

"They're coming from UNDERNEATH us," shrieked Pasqual.

"What have I done?" said Meltem.

"Stride forth," Bone commanded. "MARCH OUT AND DESTROY!"

Now the ground at the far end of the auditorium was groaning to the sound of the trumpets. Great mounds of rock began to shift and slide away, tearing against the rock around them.

Far above, Desdemona's eyes throbbed in awe. "The ground! It's openin' up! Carark!"

More of the ground buckled and folded, and an enormous section of stone foundations fell crashingly downwards.

The light shot out now, not in spindly, searching beams, but in a great wall of intense illumination.

Meltem and Pasqual half-closed their eyes against the glare of it. Jim shut one eye and tried to see through his other one.

"Look," squawked Desdemona, "the wind! The wind's rising! It's comin' from outta that big hole!"

The wind buffeted against Jim, Meltem and

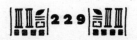

Pasqual, as strong as a mini-cyclone. It didn't start gently; it arrived with full force, tearing through the amphitheatre, screaming in and out of the hundreds of chambers and tearing across the stone benches.

"Stand firm!" yelled Jim, as Pasqual began to stagger. "Don't move, don't move an inch, or Brenda gets it!"

"Ugh," groaned Pasqual, battling to stay upright.

Bone retreated higher, into one of the more sheltered tiers of stone benches. "Come, come, COME!" he called out. "Show yourselves!"

The trumpet blaring was almost deafening; the wind merciless as it whipped all around the Colosseum, trying to flatten anything that wasn't fastened down.

Jim, Meltem and Pasqual were battling to remain standing, and breathing was getting harder and harder with the blasting wind at their faces.

And then, the thing that Bone had conjured began to emerge...

From out of the enormous chasm in the ground, to the accompaniment of countless gravelly, blaring trumpets, came a huge cloud of shimmering blueness.

Forward it moved, and the wind began to die away.

Closer it came to the centre of the Colosseum where Jim, Meltem and Pasqual were standing.

Jim stared, wide-eyed. The huge cloud began to change form, to become less hazy. Slowly Jim detected shapes in there.

"Oh, by all that's come before," he muttered. "It's ... an army!"

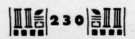

Out of the cloud emerged the spectral images of many, many men, some dressed in ancient Roman soldiers' uniforms of helmets and armour, others dressed in the torn outfits of slain gladiators. Many wore little more than rags.

The soldiers and gladiators carried spears, truncheons, long knives and other lethal-looking weapons which glinted in the blue light.

The sound of heavy marching increased, *trudge, trudge, trudge,* making the ground tremble as the spectres came closer.

None of the men had faces. All that Jim could see on top of their necks were hollowed, gaunt skulls, eyeless and grinning.

"No!" Meltem shouted. "If we don't move, they'll walk us underfoot!"

"Or CUT us DOWN with those WEAPONS!" warned Pasqual.

"Look!" yelled Jim. "See what they're carrying at the front!"

An enormous, blue, shimmering Bauble of Tiberius, the size of four men, was being held aloft by the front row of soldiers.

Jim watched as the army bore closer. He was being torn apart with indecision: if he moved out of the way, Brenda would be killed instantly, but if he, Meltem and Pasqual remained where they were, something perhaps far worse would happen to them...

Desdemona gloated high above, "Ha-crark-ha! Take a look and weep, you idiot beast. There go your friends! In another twenty seconds, them ghosts are gonna suck the life outta 'em, or flatten 'em to Kingdom Come, or—"

CLUNNNNKKKKK!

The raven teetered, and her eyes throbbed, not red this time, but with swirling stars. "Nevermore, nevermore, never—" And she fell forward, knocked out completely.

"Rark!" squawked Doris. "I've been wanting to do that for years!"

"Quaaaoooo!" snorted Brenda at the sudden arrival of her little friend, who had flown in through a hole in the wall at the back of the chamber.

"Quick, Bren, not a second to lose!" The macaw was already untying Brenda's ropes, and the Wonder Camel was shakily getting to her hoofs. "Let's get that overblown windbag!"

"QUUUUAAAAOOOOOOO!"

Now the last of the ropes was off, and Brenda was standing. She shook her humps and legs.

"Attack!" Doris screeched. In a yellow-and-blue blur, she was off.

Below, the army continued advancing.

TRUDGE, TRUDGE, TRUDGE, TRUDGE…

"NO!" shouted Pasqual.

Brenda sprang forward, leaping over the stone tiers of benches two at a time, down, down, down towards Neptune Bone.

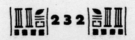

Doris got there first. She dive-bombed from the most furious height she could attain, swooping with the force of a missile towards Bone's hands.

FFFFFWWWWOOOOOOOOOOOOOOOOPPPPP!

Her beak jabbed his fingertips and she shot upwards again before he could see what had happened.

"What the – *YOWWWW!*" he screamed, dropping the Bauble onto the ground. He bent swiftly down to try and find it in the darkness.

The army was slowing, but still they came. All it would take would be for the forward flanks to lower their spears, and Jim, Meltem and Pasqual would feel the cold, hard, force of their ghostliness…

Bone's smarting fingers scrabbled across the gritty floor. Suddenly he felt something solid and hard. Something cold and tiny…

"Come to Daddy," he whispered, snatching up the Bauble.

But, before he could straighten again, Doris made another frenzied swoop. This time, Bone's enormous bottom was the target.

Doris got the bull's-eye.

"YAAAAARRRRRGGGGGHHHH!" screamed the fleshy man, jumping into the air. He was about two metres up from the floor, when Brenda the Wonder Camel lunged with all the force a Wonder Camel can muster.

"OOOOOOEEERRRRRGGGGGGHHHHHHH!" Bone went tumbling and sailing through space, flying forwards into the middle of the ghostly army.

The Bauble went flying, too – out of his hand and into the chasm.

The army stopped in its tracks. Somewhere in its midst, Neptune Bone had landed.

Suddenly, the wind rose again – sharply, as strong as the mini-cyclone it had been before. The army did not turn, but moved backwards, on and back towards the chasm.

The trumpets blared, and as the army approached the chasm, the sounds became more gravelly again.

Jim, Meltem and Pasqual watched, all of them speechless. A few tiers above, Doris and Brenda watched, squawkless and snortless.

Then, in the space of one second, the spectral marchers and all within their midst, and the wind, and the gravelly trumpet blasts – everything that had come from long ago – followed the Bauble and disappeared into the hole.

And the ground closed up around them.

Brenda, with Doris on her fore hump, made her way down to Jim and the others.

Doris got busy with the knots. "Lucky I'm an expert on ropes and things," she cooed, untying them quickly.

"Lucky you're an expert on many things," said Jim, picking her up and holding her close. He took her over to Brenda, and pressed his head against the Wonder Camel's long snout. "And lucky you're both my friends," said the archaeologist-poet.

"Quaaaoooo," Brenda snorted, in full agreement and with the inkling of a tear in one of her wide, brown eyes.

Pasqual put his arm around Meltem's shoulder and, comforting her, they followed Jim, Doris and Brenda out of the Colosseum and into the sweet, cool Roman night.

NEWS FROM PASQUAL

BACK AT CAMP in the Valley of the Kings, Cairo Jim received a letter which had been forwarded on from the Old Relics Society by Gerald Perry Esquire.

"It's from Pasqual," Jim told Doris (who had been enjoying a big meal of the freshest Malawian snails and lettuce) and Brenda (who had been immersed in the latest Melodious Tex western adventure novel). "He sent it to us, care of the Society."

Doris waddled across the table and hopped up onto Jim's shoulder. "Read it, buddy-boy," she instructed.

"Quaaaoooo," snorted Brenda.

"Righto." Jim took off his special desert sun-spectacles and read the letter to them:

"Dear Jim, Doris and Brenda the Camel of Wonder, BUONGIORNO! I hope you have RETURNED safely to your CAMPSITE after all of our EXCITE-MENT here in ROMA.

I just THOUGHT I would write and let you all KNOW about some of the OUTCOMES of our little ESCAPADE. Firstly, you will be pleased to know (but this you have probably already READ in the newspapers) that the meeting of the delegates to the

Global Total and Binding Peace Treaty of Perpetuity went ahead. But unfortunately a PRIME MINISTER or two and some KINGS and Queens did not want to be a part of it, for their OWN particular reasons. So the TREATY was not signed. Such THINGS do not surprise me, si?

Secondly, Ms BOTTNOFF has changed incredibly. I SUSPECT that the sight of what she BEHELD in the Colosseo on that fateful night jolted her OUT of whatever STATE she had fallen into. She also spent a week at a HEALTH clinic in Bolzano and is now QUITE a different person. I saw her off on a CRUISE only yesterday, and she has taken up an interest in porcelain sculptures from Burma. So it seems, my FRIENDS, she may not yet be finished with ANTIQUITIES, si?

I have ARRANGED for her to STAY and WORK here with me at the Palazzo ALTEMPS when she returns from her cruise. I have a FEELING that she will once AGAIN FLOURISH in a place such as THIS, and, besides, I look FORWARD to her company.

Thirdly, regarding BONE. Well, no one has SEEN sight nor SMELT odour of him since that same night. It SEEMS he has vanished off the FACE of the EARTH. As for his raven, the Antiquities Squad searched all OVER the Colosseo for HER, but could find not EVEN a feather. May it be the LAST we ever see of that SKULDUGGEROUS pair, si?

Lastly, I should LIKE to share something with YOU,

but you must promise NEVER to tell another SOUL of this (people are only too QUICK to jump into conclusions, si?). Well, the other NIGHT I was alone, doing my rounds of the Altemps, when, in the OBELISK Room, what do you THINK should happen? There was a VOICE ... and it SANG! It sang to ME! After so LONG, my friends, I HEAR it! And this is what it sang:

> *The Past will last*
> *The now is here*
> *things misjudged*
> *are now all clear*
> *and History is built on such*
> *hearts, minds and souls –*
> *protect them much.*

The strange thing is, my FRIENDS, the VOICE. It sounded like a VOICE I have heard sometime in my YOUTH ... a woman's voice, LOW and DEEP and very VERY APPEALING.

Well, now I go. I HOPE we shall all meet AGAIN, but next TIME under less WINDY circumstances. Ciao!

I REMAIN your good FRIEND,

Pasqual."

Cairo Jim put down the letter. "It's like I've often thought," he said. "The secrets are out there. And sometimes they're *within* as well."

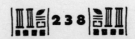

And Doris *raaarrrk*ed happily in his ear, and Brenda *quaaaooo*ed contentedly by his side.

And still the smell of oily roses, faintly tinged with kerosene, filled the campsite, and wafted ever onwards to the Valley of the Kings.

THE END

▲ ▲ ▲ ▲ ▲ ▲ ▲ ▲ ▲ ▲ ▲ ▲ ▲ ▲ ▲ ▲ ▲ ▲ ▲

The Ventriloquist's Alphabet from
Ventriloquism for Fun and Profit in Confined Spaces
by Sebastian Orgling

Keep the lips slightly parted for the best effect.

Normal	Ventriloquism	Normal	Ventriloquism
a	a	n	n
b	d	o	o
c	c	p	t
d	d	q	q
e	e	r	r
f	eth	s	s
g	g	t	t
h	h	u	u
i	i	v	thee
j	j	w	duggl-u
k	k	x	x
l	l	y	y
m	n	z	z

▲ ▲ ▲ ▲ ▲ ▲ ▲ ▲ ▲ ▲ ▲ ▲ ▲ ▲ ▲ ▲ ▲ ▲ ▲

Swoggle me sideways!
Unearth more thrilling mysteries
of history starring Cairo Jim, Doris,
and Brenda the Wonder Camel –

THE CAIRO JIM
CHRONICLES

The Cairo Jim Chronicles,
read by Geoffrey McSkimming,
are available on CD
from Bolinda Audio Books!
See **www.bolinda.com** for details.